Who Will Speak
for the Lamb?

By the Same Author

CONJURING SUMMER IN

Who Will Speak for the Lamb?

by Mildred Ames

HARPER & ROW, PUBLISHERS
Cambridge, Philadelphia, St. Louis, San Francisco,
London, Singapore, Sydney, Tokyo
NEW YORK

Typography by Joyce Hopkins
1 2 3 4 5 6 7 8 9 10
First Edition

Library of Congress Cataloging-in-Publication Data
Ames, Mildred.
  Who will speak for the lamb? / by Mildred Ames.
    p.   cm.
  Summary: Although at first antagonistic to one another, high school senior and
former model Julie and college freshman Jeff find their mutual interest in an
activist group fighting for animal rights gives both of them a chance to become
individuals in the shadow of domineering mothers.
  ISBN 0-06-020111-8 : $ ISBN 0-06-020112-6 (lib. bdg.) : $
  [1. Animals—Treatment—Fiction.   2. Mothers—Fiction.
3. Identity—Fiction.]   I. Title.
PZ7.A5143Who 1989   88-21208
[Fic]—dc19   CIP
                                                                        AC

To my old friends,
Lorrie and John Durante

Prologue

All eyes were glued to the front of the agricultural science classroom where Mr. Davis, wearing a heavy apron, had one knee embedded in a mass of gray, woolly fur belonging to a lamb stretched over a crude bench.

"You'll notice," he said, "that I've tied the two front legs to a hind leg. That prevents struggling which could cause you to bruise the carcass. You don't want that."

The lamb gave a sharp bleat.

Mr. Davis said, "Now this isn't the method they use in slaughterhouses, naturally. It's the way farmers do it. In the left hand, hold the animal's nose, careful not to cut off breathing. Stretch out the neck." He held a knife in his right hand. "Push the knife through the neck, close to the neck bone, just behind the angle of the jaw and below the base of the ear." He took the sharp tip and pointed to the area. "In slitting a lamb's throat, the cut can be made either away from or toward the neck bone."

The lamb struggled against the ropes that tied its legs but without success. A shrill cry issued from its throat. Instantly,

Mr. Davis, with a firm thrust, drove his knife deep into the animal's neck and blood spurted out all over his apron.

As the lamb's death throes subsided to a twitching, he said, "Now the neck should be broken. You grasp the nose with the left hand so, and the wool on the face between the lamb's eyes with the right. Pull the nose up and push down hard with the heel of the right hand on the lamb's face."

When he finished, he wiped his hands carefully on his already heavily bloodstained apron.

1

This has got to be one of the longest days of my life, Julie thought, as the end of her first day at Kennedy High neared. Her father had requested that none of her teachers call undue attention to her. She was simply to be Julie Peters, new student. Although they had honored the request, word spread quickly anyhow. People sneaked glances at her, but if she looked at them, they turned quickly away. They pointed at her, whispered about her, but none of them spoke to her.

She told herself that as a model she was used to being an object of attention but in a different way—as a commodity. She knew she responded automatically to the collective group of professionals who said words of approval like *wonderful, beautiful, terrific*—but all that had nothing to do with relating to individuals.

At the end of the day, as she retrieved her suede jacket from her locker, she thought, It's no good. I'll never be able to fit in. They all think I'm some kind of freak.

A voice beside her said, "You really *are* Julie Peters, the model, aren't you? I didn't believe it at first."

Julie glanced over to find a girl she recognized from one of her classes, a girl who had looked so familiar Julie had the feeling that she must have met her someplace before. Now that someone had finally spoken to her, Julie didn't know quite how to respond, so she smiled and nodded.

"I'm Laura Ryder," the girl said. "My mother sold you your house."

Of course. Laura was the image of her mother, with the same very black hair, fair skin, and blue eyes. "I feel as though I should have known you," Julie said. "You look so much like your mother."

"We both do—my brother Jeff and I. Jeff says we're living proof that the Spanish were guilty of a lot of hanky-panky with the Irish." Laura gave a winning grin. "You know, you look like your pictures and yet you don't. I can't figure out what's different."

Julie knew only too well. None of the models she'd worked with had really looked like their photographs. Some even looked ordinary, yet they were the chosen few who brought some kind of magic to the camera. Not any pretty face could do it, Morgan Slade, Julie's agent, was fond of saying. People outside the business rarely ever understood that and to explain sounded like boasting. "It's probably from the lack of makeup."

Laura gave that some thought, then finally said, "Yeah, I guess that must be it. You know, I told my mother you just couldn't be the same Julie Peters because why would a top model like you want to come to a hick town like Santa Delores."

Julie said quickly, "My father is a psychology professor. The university offered him a chance to do some research he's wanted to do for a long time. We'd all been wanting a change from New York anyhow, so my mother and I came with him." That was only a half-truth, but she wasn't about to tell more than that to someone she'd just met.

"How will you do your modeling from here?" Laura asked.

"I won't," Julie said, feeling upset by all the questions. Then she chided herself for being overly sensitive. Perhaps the girl was only trying to be friendly. She added, "Right now I have to put all my efforts into trying to prepare for college."

"I know what you mean. It sure doesn't leave much time for anything that's fun." Laura pulled a sweater from her locker, put it on, and just as Julie was about to leave, said, "I've been asking everybody in school if they'd join our demonstration today. Would you think I was too pushy if I asked you?"

"I don't think I understand."

Laura clicked her tongue and rolled her eyes. "Talk about stupid—that's me. How could you understand? You weren't even here when they did it. That was almost a week ago. They slaughtered a lamb in one of the agricultural science classes. At least, that's what they called it. I call it murder. They slit the poor thing's throat right in front of everybody in the room."

Julie couldn't believe her ears. Was the girl telling the truth? One look at the expression on her face said she was. Slaughtered a lamb in class? What kind of a school was this anyhow?

Laura said, "Just because a lot of the kids come in from farms outside town, they think that makes it okay to start some kind of butchering class. What's even worse is that so many of the kids agree. They say I'm overreacting."

Julie shivered. She remembered the Christmas of the first

3

year she'd worked with Morgan. She was eleven then. Morgan, because she always called Julie "Lamb Chop," had made her the gift of a woolly stuffed lamb. Even though Julie had felt she was too old for stuffed toys, she had loved that soft, huggable creature. She still had it. *They slit the poor thing's throat.* "How monstrous!" she said.

Laura said. "I thought you'd feel like that! Then you'll demonstrate with us."

The words were a declaration, not a question. "Demonstrate?"

"Yes. You must have seen us this morning. We were out in front of school, carrying signs."

"I guess I missed you. I had to come early to get oriented."

Laura linked her arm through Julies's. "Come on. A lot of us feel just the way you do. It *was* a monstrous thing to do, and there's only one way to make the powers-that-be understand that we are just not going to stand by and let barbaric acts like that take place in our school."

Before Julie was fully aware of what was happening, Laura had gently led her out the door and through a group of people carrying signs and parading up and down in front of the school, then over to a young man who seemed to be organizing people into lines.

Laura said, "Jeff, this is Julie Peters. She wants to join the cause. Julie, my brother, Jeff. Lucky for us he's in the Animal Rights Society."

Like Laura, he strongly resembled his mother except that he must have been well over six feet. His sister, had she been a model, would have belonged in petites.

"Hi," Jeff said to Julie, staring at her in the way she'd come to hate. Is it or isn't it the real Julie Peters? the look always seemed to say.

4

"How about giving us our signs," Laura said to him.

Jeff handed over his own to Julie. She glanced at the words "High School Is Not the Place to Teach Violence" and took the sign from him. "I'll get a couple more from the car," he told Laura.

"Okay, I'll go with you." Laura turned to Julie. "Just get in the line, Julie, and I'll be with you in a minute."

Feeling foolish, Julie took a place behind a couple who looked much too old to be high school students. Then she noticed that some of the signs bore the name *Animal Rights Society*. Obviously Jeff's doing.

She had mixed emotions about the whole thing. On the one hand, she could see humor in the situation. This was only her first day in school and here she was, doing something she had never dreamed of doing before: militantly demonstrating on behalf of a Cause. Often she had seen pictures on television of people. young and old, standing together for what they believed in, even sometimes going to jail. She had wondered how it would feel to join with others in a common cause, to be brave like a Jane Fonda, fighting for what you thought was right.

She glanced around at the others, and as they gave her welcoming smiles, feelings of warmth and camaraderie began to flood through her. Was this what life could be like for people who were a part of the real world? How good that seemed!

She thought of how often she and Dr. Almquist, the psychiatrist she'd been seeing until recently, had talked about her need to learn how to do things on her own. But she was so used to her mother's guiding her life, arranging for aerobics classes, dance instruction, voice lessons—everything. How could you suddenly turn all that around and take charge?

And when he'd asked her what she thought she'd like to do with her life, she'd drawn a complete blank. Julie, the robot, evidently had to be programmed by someone else.

"You have to begin making some decisions for yourself, Julie," he had said. "They needn't be big decisions—career decisions or life decisions. Start small. Maybe you'd like to learn how to roller skate or take an art class or wear funky clothes—whatever. When the urge hits you, go with it. And don't let anyone talk you out of it!"

Her eyes took in the protest marchers. Of course, the decision to join them had been more Laura's than hers. Nevertheless she was doing something completely out of character. Dr. Almquist would have been proud of her.

She looked around for Laura and spotted her and Jeff talking beside a white Mustang parked a little way up the street. Laura was pointing toward the group of demonstrators and chatting excitedly away. Jeff's gaze followed her hand and, Julie was almost sure, rested on her. She wondered what Laura was saying. *She really is Julie Peters?* Probably. Julie began to feel the same warm glow for Laura and Jeff that she had felt for the others. Comrades. Sharing a cause.

A few minutes later Laura joined her and said, "Jeff had to find a phone to make a call. He'll be right back."

Twenty minutes must have passed before Jeff returned and took a place beside Laura. Not five minutes later a car screeched up to the curb near the demonstrators and two men hopped out, one with a camera. Julie could just make out a card inside the windshield that said *Press*. In another moment she heard one of the men say, "Where's Julie Peters?"

The other man spotted her and said, "There she is. Come on."

How could they have found out? In a flash Julie knew beyond a doubt. That was what Laura and Jeff were talking about at the car, and that was why Jeff had to leave to make a phone call. How could I have been so stupid? Julie asked herself. The real world was no different from the fantasy world. Both used you. Her eyes smarted with angry tears. When a reporter grabbed her arm, she snapped, "Don't you dare touch me!" and wrenched free to tear away from him and head back toward school.

"And you were the one who wanted to keep such a low profile," Anne Peters said to Julie at breakfast the next morning. She studied the picture on the front page of the Santa Delores *Times* and shook her head.

Julie was aware of the heavy note of sarcasm in her mother's voice. She was also aware that no matter how much her mother tried to hide her feelings, she was still deeply resentful that Julie had, for the moment, turned her back on a highly successful modeling career.

Anne passed the paper to Julie's father, who glanced at it as he drank coffee. Harrison Peters's eyes glinted with amusement. "It would seem that you simply are not destined to escape the limelight, my girl," he said to Julie.

"Dad, I had nothing to do with this. It was Noreen Ryder's daughter. She set me up. I know she did."

"Noreen Ryder? Our real estate agent?" he asked.

"Yes." Julie told him about meeting Laura and about how the girl had persuaded her to join the protest over the slaughtered lamb. "Then this boy, Jeff, had to make a telephone

7

call and a few minutes later the reporters showed up. It was awful."

Her father reached over and patted her hand. "The price of fame, I'm afraid."

"I told you she should have a bodyguard, but you wouldn't listen," her mother said.

"Anne, that's the last thing she needs. Remember what Dr. Almquist said?"

"I know, I know—no glitter, no fanfare. We're all to lead an ordinary, uneventful, drab family life."

"*Uneventful* and *drab* are your words, not the psychiatrist's. Julie needs the chance to learn what it feels like to be a teenager. She needs a taste of the real world."

As her mother and father discussed her as if she weren't in the room, Julie studied them both. Her mother was still a handsome woman, tall and queenly, Julie thought. *She* should have been the model. She loved that world, loved the junkets abroad, loved the glamor, loved the spotlight, all of which she could experience only through Julie.

Julie knew she strongly resembled her mother. She had the same height, the same ash-blond hair (although hers was not frosted), and the same wide, gray eyes. She could find the resemblance in all of her photographs, and she hated it. It made her feel that she was nothing but a younger Anne, living her mother's dream life.

"My mother *could* have done for me what I've done for you," her mother was fond of saying. "It just never even occurred to her. And it never occurred to me that I was good model material until after I was married. Then you came along, and by that time it was too late to get a foot in the door. You have to start young."

And, indeed, her mother had started her young. She was eight years old when she got her first modeling assignment as one of six little girls chosen for a mother and daughter matching-dress spread for *McCall's* magazine. By the time she'd turned thirteen she had developed into what her mother called "real model material." From that point on, all their lives had taken a complete turnabout. They'd left the New Jersey town where she was born to buy an apartment in New York City. Her father had given up a job in research, which he'd loved, to take a straight teaching job, which he'd hated, at Columbia University. And all to give young Julie Peters her great chance. She thought now, If only Anne's mother had done for Anne what Anne has done for me, I might have been spared.

She gazed fondly at her father, glad he was at last doing work he liked. If only she had looked like him, life would have been so different. He was not handsome by any means, yet she supposed he could be called distinguished. Certainly her mother would have settled for nothing less than distinguished. At Columbia, he had grown a beard and mustache which he said he hoped would make him look professorial. If anything, his full head of dark hair along with the bushy black beard and mustache made him look forbidding. If *distinguished* wasn't quite the right word, *interesting* certainly was. Interesting and intense. Her mother always chose his clothes, soft cashmere jackets, flannel trousers, silk shirts. Left to his own devices, he would have lived in jeans, yet he wore her choices good-naturedly.

Her mother had also chosen this large, imposing home, complete with swimming pool and tennis court. When Julie said, "Why do we need something so big?" Anne answered,

"You forget who you are. You have to keep up appearances. When you have interviews, they always describe your surroundings. You know that. Besides, the pool and the tennis court are just what you need to keep your body in shape."

Somehow her mother just couldn't seem to understand that the last thing Julie wanted was more interviews. She'd had enough to last a lifetime. Although the place seemed ostentatious to her, she couldn't begrudge her mother's choice. The house, Julie knew, was only a poor substitute for the suspended modeling career her mother had taken so much gratification from. Julie's money had paid for the place, but she couldn't begrudge that either. Although she had earned a considerable amount, her mother had shrewdly invested everything not needed for expenses. Julie's worth had grown to what her family would have once thought of as "untold wealth." If anyone deserved a big piece of the pie, it was her mother.

Julie was suddenly aware that her father was talking to her. "I have to agree with those kids that slaughtering animals in a high school classroom hardly seems appropriate," he was saying, "and you've got to realize that people will take advantage of your name—or maybe I should say your celebrity—it if will promote their causes. It's up to you whether or not you want to let them. It's probably a good thing this happened. From now on you'll be more aware of where your actions can lead. If you don't want to see your picture in the paper, don't involve yourself in other people's schemes."

"Don't worry, I won't."

Her mother picked up the newspaper and eyed it thoughtfully. "What's that saying about an ill wind? You know"— she pointed to Julie's picture—"this won't hurt. It shows great sympathy—caring for defenseless animals, that sort of thing. I'm sure the national press will pick up on it. It will help keep your face before the public. You don't want them to forget you entirely before you go back to work."

Julie silently groaned. Just the thought of that day made her feel sick.

2

That same morning at breakfast, Noreen Ryder eyed the protest picture in the Santa Delores *Times* and said to Jeff and Laura, "Well, I guess you two must have done something right to make the front page. And I don't mind saying that my calling around to rally support didn't do any harm either."

I could have just as easily done it myself, Jeff thought, then immediately felt guilty for begrudging his mother a part in the affair. She needed to feel involved in something vital and important. And what could be more important than the Animal Rights Society, a group his father had helped organize? Only recently Jeff had joined, mostly to please her. She seemed to think that, as a family, they owed it to his dad's memory.

She interrupted his thoughts with "Aren't you going to thank me for all my work?"

"Oh, sure—sure. You were a big help, Mom," he said. "As for Laura and me—well, we were only doing what Dad would have wanted us to do."

Laura added, "Dad always said that the only way to change things was to speak out—protest."

"I know," Noreen said. "And I'm very proud of you. Your dad was an idealist, and I loved him for it." Her eyes filled with tears. "Sometimes I think it was his idealism that killed him."

Jeff knew what she was referring to. When his dad had needed surgery to replace a defective heart valve, rather than accept one taken from a healthy pig he had opted for a man-made device. Although his doctors claimed they had given him as accurate an assessment of the choices as they could at the time, within a year it had failed. Supposedly the pig valve would have lasted many years longer. But who was to say that that wouldn't have failed too? In any case, his dad had been a firm believer that one species should not be sacrificed to another, so he probably would not have acted differently under any circumstances.

Glancing again at the newspaper article, Noreen said, "I see you wasted no time in recruiting Julie Peters. I had no idea she was *that* famous. The paper makes it sound as if she was the only person in the protest march."

Laura snorted. "I know. They were more interested in her than in the purpose for the whole thing."

Noreen asked, "Was it her idea to demonstrate with you?"

"No," Laura said. "I asked her. But she was agreeable. We would never have made the paper without her."

"Oh?" Noreen said.

"Yes. Jeff just happened to mention yesterday how we'd get a lot more attention if we had a celebrity like Cleveland Amory to demonstrate with us. I didn't think another thing about it until I introduced Julie to Jeff. In fact, it was Jeff who hit on the idea then."

13

Jeff grinned. "Brilliant me. When Laura told me she was really *the* Julie Peters, it dawned on me that we had our own Cleveland Amory after all, so I called the paper right away."

"I hope you asked her permission first."

The thought had fleetingly occurred to him, but he'd put it aside. She might have said no. The demonstration was important to him. This was the first one he'd planned by himself, and he wanted it to be so successful that everyone would say, *Your dad couldn't have done better.* Maybe that would appease his mother.

But the memory of how the two reporters had snapped all those pictures of Julie, then descended upon her, firing questions, made Jeff have second thoughts now. He could still see the expression on her face as she turned and fled back toward school and almost into the arms of Mr. Webber, the principal, as he was leaving the building. He took her quickly inside and warded off her two pursuers.

"Jeff, did you ask the girl?" his mother persisted.

Jeff put the disturbing picture out of his head and said, "I figure that anyone who goes in for a career like hers has got to love publicity."

Noreen said, "Only this time she wasn't paid for it."

Jeff shrugged. "Do her good. This is probably the only time she's ever used her fame to do something for someone besides herself."

"How can you be so hard on her?" Laura said. "You don't even know her."

"She's a model, isn't she? They're all the same—narcissistic. All they're concerned with is their looks."

Noreen got up and started clearing away the dirty dishes. "It doesn't matter what she's like. I still think you should have asked her permission. After all, I got a handsome commission because of the Peterses. I'd hate them to be annoyed with us."

His mother had worked hard for her real estate license after his father's death. It was helping to support them now so that the bulk of the insurance money could go toward Laura's and his college educations. Even so, using Julie Peters had done more good than bad. Look at the publicity the ARS had received.

"Mom's right," Laura said. "We should have asked."

"Too late now," he said.

"You'd better apologize as soon as possible," Noreen said to Laura. "Tell the girl your brother thought you'd already asked her for permission."

Jeff said, "Laura can apologize if she wants to, but as far as I'm concerned, she doesn't have to lie about it. I don't care what Julie Peters thinks."

Noreen said, "Well, I do. At least, I care what her parents think. I wouldn't want them to imagine that we're trying to hurt their daughter."

"No one was trying to hurt her," Jeff said with irritation. "But if it will make you feel any better, maybe Laura can apologize for both of us."

"That's better," Noreen said.

Laura said, "I'll apologize, but I think I'll blame it all on you, Jeff. *You* don't have to go to school with her."

He could see the twinkle in her eyes, but he didn't care if Julie Peters *did* blame him. He had more important things to worry about. "So be it," he said, through with the subject.

He scanned the article again. "After they get through talking about her, they finally get to the purpose of the

15

protest." He read from the paper. " 'School officials defended the butchering demonstration, saying that even the SPCA admits there is nothing illegal about slaughtering animals in the classroom. However, Laura Ryder, who led the protest march, said, "Killing that poor creature was an outrage." When asked how she felt about dissecting animals in school, she responded, "I don't think it's educational or humane. Kids can just as easily learn from video tapes or models." ' "

Jeff agreed with her. Most kids in science classes were never going to do anything that would require knowledge of dissecting any creature. In *his* chosen profession it was different, though. He would have to have this learning. He knew of cases where whole flocks of animals had been dying from unknown causes. When that happened, a wild-life biologist had to do on-the-spot dissections to discover what was killing them before he could save the others. A few had to be sacrificed for the many. That bothered him.

Noreen, who was loading the dishwasher now, glanced over her shoulder and said, "Your father would be proud of both of you." She smiled warmly. "Speaking of your father reminds me that the first concert of the season is starting next Saturday. You know how he loved the symphony. We hardly ever missed a week. I think it would be awfully nice if you both went with me, at least this time anyhow."

"Oh, Mom," Laura said. "You should have said something sooner. I already have plans that I can't change."

Smart old Laura, Jeff thought, she always has plans she can't change. He envied her in more ways than that one. Laura planned to major in art in college, so no one would badger her into attending old Santa Delores U, the small local university where their father had taught botany and where Jeff was now a freshman. All the good art schools were elsewhere. Lucky her.

Originally he'd wanted to go to a different and larger university in another town himself, but his mother had talked him out of it. "Laura and I need you here this year, Jeff," she'd said. "With your father gone, we can use your moral support—not to mention your company. Besides, you'll be able to save money living at home."

"This year" was turning into forever. She fully expected him to put in three more years at Santa Delores and graduate as a wild-life biologist. Now he wasn't at all sure that that was what he wanted to do with his life. Lately his thoughts kept returning to last summer when he'd worked in his Uncle Dan's law office in San Francisco and loved every minute of it. "If you went to Stanford," his uncle had said, "you could work here part-time all year round. Palo Alto isn't all that far." The idea seemed more and more appealing, but when he'd broached the subject to his mother, she'd grown very upset.

She broke into his thoughts now. "How about you, Jeff? You'll go with me, won't you?"

"Go with you?"

"To the concert. Weren't you listening?"

"Oh—the concert. Well—" He wanted to tell her the truth, that between his studies, her demands, and cranking out bagels for his part-time job at the Bagel Machine, he was just keeping his head above water.

Before he could say a word, she added, "I miss your dad so much when things like this come up. I'd never dream of going alone."

Jeff swallowed hard, then said, "Sure, Mom. Sure. I'll go with you."

17

Right after Laura had left for school, Noreen said, "I think Laura is seeing too much of Brian. I know they do a lot of studying together, but four times a week is just too much. I think you should talk to her, Jeff."

Jeff bristled. "Why me?"

"Because I always seem to prick her the wrong way. But she listens to you, just the way she did to Dad. He could get her to do anything. You're a lot like him, Jeff."

"I'll see what I can do."

"You're such a comfort to me," his mother said.

Jeff could understand and sympathize with his mother's loneliness. But it was two years now. How long could loneliness last?

The immediate concerns of demanding classes pushed all domestic issues to the back of Jeff's mind until he returned home that afternoon. Laura was already there, and from the look of her, thoroughly disturbed. She sat in the kitchen, an untouched glass of fruit juice in front of her. Instead of drinking it, she stared, glassy-eyed, at a wrinkled piece of paper in her hand.

As Jeff took a carton of milk from the refrigerator and poured himself a glass, all the time thinking of how he was supposed to lecture her, she thrust the paper under his nose. "Just look at that!" she said, obviously close to tears.

Jeff set down his glass on the table, took the paper from her hand, and read:

> "Laura had a little lamb.
> Its fleece was white as snow,
> And every place that Laura went,
> The lamb was sure to go.

It followed her to school one day
To see what students do;
They butchered it in science class,
And Laura had lamb stew."

Jeff shook his head. "That's pretty childish. Don't let it get to you."

"That's easy for you to say. You don't have to face these kids every day." Tears started to fill her eyes and roll down her cheeks now. She grunted as if annoyed with herself, got up, stamped over to the paper-towel holder, yanked off a section, and dabbed at her eyes. "This has just got to be the rottenest day of my life." Apparently reconsidering, she added, "Well, one of the rottenest anyhow."

He could see that she wanted to talk about her rotten day. If his father had been alive he would have been there for her, but as he wasn't—well, what were big brothers for anyhow? "What happened?" he asked.

She poured out the whole story. First, there was the argument with Brian. Laura said, "I asked him why he'd told me about the lamb in the first place if he didn't want me to do something about it. After all, I don't take agricultural science—he does. Brian said he didn't expect anyone to make that big a deal out of it. He said all the kids think I'm a dingbat. I said, 'I don't care what all the kids think. What do you think?' He said, 'I think you're trying to be Joan of Arc or something.' Imagine—Joan of Arc!"

Hoping to mollify her, Jeff said, "Some people think Joan of Arc was trying to do something important."

A look of dawning washed over her face. "You're right! I wish I'd thought of that. And something else I should have said—if the kids in that class want to be butchers, they should go to some special school."

Jeff smiled. She seemed very young to him at that moment, very vulnerable. He knew he was supposed to talk to her about seeing Brian too much, but that seemed unimportant just now. "You and Brian have had spats before. He'll get over it."

Laura's eyes blazed. "I don't care if he does. If two people don't think the same things are important, they can't have a meaningful relationship."

She sounded so melodramatic that Jeff almost smiled. He caught himself though. His dad would never have treated her problems lightly. He said, "I'm sorry, Laura, I guess you have had a lousy day."

She groaned. "That's only the beginning. On top of that, our nerdy principal had to give me a lecture."

"Mr. Webber?"

"The same."

"What did he want?"

"Well, he really lit into me in that sticky way he has, with a smile on his lips the whole time."

"I remember," Jeff said.

"He told me he definitely upholds my First Amendment right to protest because that's what democracy is all about. However—and it was that however that did me in." She quoted, using a deep voice, " 'However we all have a responsibility for using good sense, Laura, and *that* is what you didn't do. You should have come to me with your grievance first.' "

"And just what would he have done?"

"He called it a misunderstanding that he could have

20

straightened out in short order. He accused me of preferring to grandstand it.''

"Sometimes that's the only way of gaining attention.'' Jeff was starting to feel responsible for Laura's plight. After all, he was the one who had suggested demonstrating, and now she had to take the abuse that probably should have been aimed at him.

Laura sat down and took a sip of her juice. "He told me that Mr. Davis was one of the school's most gifted teachers and then went into a whole big thing about learning first-hand instead of just through books and a lot of other stuff like that. Then, finally, he said, 'I'm not going to make a big deal out of this. I respect your beliefs as I would your religion. You are entitled to them. But, remember, other people are entitled to theirs too.' Then he sent me back to class.''

"I'm afraid this is all my fault,'' Jeff said. "I didn't mean to make trouble for you.''

Laura gave a deep sigh. "I think it's all for the best. At least I found out what Brian's made of. All he cares about is what other people think.''

"Is this going to make a difference between you two?''

"Of course it makes a difference. He insulted me on the ride home, calling me a dingbat. I got out of his car and told him I was walking. And he let me! He said to call him when I come to my senses. That'll be the day!''

Jeff breathed a sigh of relief. He wouldn't have to give Laura a talking-to about seeing Brian too much after all. If there was one thing she didn't need that afternoon, it was another lecture.

He was sorry his idea of demonstrating had caused her so

21

many problems. Nevertheless, if he had it to do over again, he would have done the same. After all, nothing would have stopped his dad if what he did was for the cause, even though he'd had to keep a very low profile because of his job. The university had an animal research program that the ARS disapproved of and were often vocal about. The organization thought his father could be more effective if he kept his membership secret. The same was true of Jeff.

Jeff thought now of how the members of the Animal Rights Society who had joined them for the march had thumped him on the back afterward and said, "You're following right along in your dad's footsteps." He couldn't imagine why that didn't make him feel more elated than it did. Certainly he cared just as much about "the cause" as his father had. Yet lately he was starting to feel that the likeness between the two of them ended there.

3

"I'll come right to the point, Miss Peters—or Julie, if I may," Mr. Webber said. His lips parted in what, Julie assumed, was meant to be a fatherly smile.

Julie said nothing. This was only her third day at Kennedy High, but she felt just as uncomfortable as she had the first day, if not more so. She wondered if she was becoming paranoid. All day long she'd noticed that whenever she passed a group of chattering students they suddenly fell silent, almost as if they had been talking about her. And now she'd been called to the principal's office. In books, that always indicated that you'd committed some serious offense.

She was certain that all of today's problems were arising out of that stupid protest march. She waited anxiously for Mr. Webber to confirm her suspicions and . . . And what? Throw her out of school? Still, there *was* that fatherly smile. Or was it just a mouth frozen open, like a gargoyle's?

Mr. Webber said, "I understand, Julie, that, for the biggest part of your life, you've been privately tutored. Is that right?"

"Yes," she said, trying to look more composed than she felt.

"Of course you have," he said.

Then why did you ask? she thought.

"And, naturally, we have to expect some difficulties in adjusting to the academic environment for the first time, don't we?"

Insurmountable difficulties, Julie thought. She said, "I didn't expect killing an animal in a classroom to be one of them."

"This is the first year that's been done here. Mr. Davis, the teacher, cleared it with me first. It was an experiment and one that he would probably do in only one class a year.

"You have to understand, Julie, that the majority of his students come from farms outside town. They are accustomed to viewing animals in a different light. If nothing else, they're used to seeing chickens or turkeys or geese killed. Some of them have probably handled the job themselves." He gave a little laugh. "Oh, sure, we all hate to think of what goes on in slaughterhouses, but we all like our Big Macs now and then, don't we?"

Julie said nothing.

"As I was saying, quite often, when we're placed in a new environment, we don't know exactly what's expected of us. And if no one guides us or makes the rules clear, then we can't be blamed for little missteps, can we?"

He was implying that she had been raised in a bubble. And he was right. Confronting the world outside that germ-free atmosphere now, in the form of this benignly smiling man, terrified her. "If you mean about the demonstration—that was a terrible mistake. It really wasn't my idea. And I had nothing to do with the newspaper story. I mean, I really didn't know what I was getting into."

24

"Of course you didn't. Why, even your parents advised me that in no way did you want to be the center of attention. So we must rule out that possibility. Besides, that was your first day here. How could you have any idea of what all the hoopla was about? I would imagine you thought it was sort of a lark?"

Was he giving her an out? "I guess I did—then."

"Of course you did. All perfectly natural. And yet, look at the result of that little lark. A trifling matter has been blown up out of all proportion, mostly, I suspect, because the name Julie Peters has given the whole issue an importance it would never have otherwise commanded."

Julie swallowed hard. "I'm sorry, Mr. Webber. I don't know how I even got into the thing. Someone asked me if I would and the next thing I knew, there I was out there with a sign and—"

"Someone asked you—Laura Ryder, I suppose?" When Julie failed to respond, he added, "A most persuasive young lady, I suspect. But, no matter. What you must realize, Julie, whether you like it or not, is you are bound to be a role model for many young women in this country, including your classmates. That's a great responsibility and one you must never misuse. Do you understand?"

Of course she understood. When she had come to Santa Delores she'd thought she had shed a great burden—for the time being anyhow. Now he was placing another just as great on her shoulders. She had to be some paragon of perfection for the benefit not only of her classmates, but of all the faceless young women in the country. I can't do it, she thought. I just can't do it. It was all a mistake, coming here, imagining I could find a place for myself, even imagining I might, at last, find out who I really am. Without think-

25

ing, she murmured, "It was a mistake—a terrible mistake."

"Of course it was," Mr. Webber said. "And everyone is entitled to one mistake. Now we'll say no more about it. I'm sure there will be no repeat. As they say, a word to the wise is sufficient."

As he dismissed Julie, the thought occurred to her that he had smiled through their whole encounter. She had visions of his disappearing like the Cheshire cat, leaving his smile behind.

Although Laura Ryder shared two of Julie's classes that day, Julie went out of her way to avoid eye contact with her. Fortunately, after each class, her teachers had detained Julie to find out if she needed boning up on the first semester's work. Much to Julie's relief, the delays had left no possibility for words with Laura.

And what would she say anyhow? She had never been able to express simple anger, let alone rage. All her life she had been trained to please. When she had been a little girl, before each photographing session, her mother would say, "Remember, Julie, sparkle," and Julie would look into the camera and think of bright, shooting rays and glittering stars, until she lit up and sparkled for her mother. Julie Peters, she thought, the trained sparkler. No, there was just no way she could tell Laura how mad and hurt and used she'd felt. All she could do was try to avoid her.

By the end of the school day, Julie felt thoroughly despondent. She wanted to go home and say, *It's just not working. I don't belong there. I can't fit in. I'm a freak.* Yet, if she did, she knew exactly what her mother would say: "Well, I'm glad you've come to your senses. Of course you don't

26

belong in a public school. Tomorrow we'll find you a tutor," and Julie would know that she was a failure as a human being.

She ended the day in the school library, stalling until she was certain the majority of students had left and she would not run into Laura Ryder. Finally, she decided the coast had to be clear, so she headed for her locker to get her things and return to the library to kill time until her mother picked her up.

Along the way, a few stragglers chatted about concerns that seemed far removed from the world of Julie Peters. She hurried past them with only one thought in mind—to get her jacket and escape. When she had almost reached her locker she realized that the one person she had tried so hard to miss was standing in front of it, obviously waiting for her. Julie wanted to turn around and run, but Laura Ryder had already seen her.

"Hi," Laura said. "I've been waiting here forever. I was beginning to think I'd missed you."

Julie said a curt *Hi,* then gave all her attention to opening her locker, taking out her jacket, and slipping into it. Everything she wanted to say to Laura remained stuck in her throat.

"Mind if I walk out with you?" Laura asked.

Normally Julie would have said *Of course not,* but she thought of Dr. Almquist's words. "What do you think will happen to you if you tell people how you feel? What are you afraid of, Julie?"

"I don't know," she told him. "I guess I'm afraid they'll get mad—that they won't like what I've said."

"They won't like what you've said? Or they won't like you?"

27

She'd known what he was doing. They had been over the same ground before. Always it came back to one thing. She was so afraid people wouldn't like her that she could never express herself honestly. But did she really care what Laura thought of her? After yesterday? No way.

Even so, she had to take a deep breath before she turned to Laura and said, "Why do you want to walk out with me? Do you have some other plan for using me the way you did the other day?"

For a moment Laura looked stricken, then she recovered, and said, "I've been waiting all day to apologize to you. I just wanted you to know that I consider myself as much to blame as my brother, Jeff, even though he was the one who called the newspaper. My mother said we should have asked your permission, and she was right. Sometimes, I'm afraid, both of us tend to act first and think later, especially when it's for the cause."

"The cause?"

"Yes, you see—well, it's kind of a long story." She paused as if she didn't know where to begin. "Look, there's a deli not far from here where we can get a Coke or something. We can talk there and I'll try to apologize properly. How about it?"

Julie hesitated. The girl looked sincerely sorry. Yet the hurt of that first day was still so painful that she found it hard to be forgiving.

"Please come," Laura said. "I think I know how you feel, and I don't blame you, but *I* won't feel right until I know you're not mad at me anymore."

Realizing that her anger was now ebbing, Julie said, "I'm not mad at you. After all, you didn't force me to go out and carry a sign. I'm a big girl. I could have said no. And if *you* didn't call the paper, then I don't have a reason to be mad at you. I can't say the same for your brother though."

Laura laughed. "I don't care if you're mad at him, just so's you're not mad at me. And if you're not mad at me, you'll show it by letting me treat you. Okay?"

Why not? Her mother planned to pick her up every day after school, but Julie had already called home that afternoon to say she needed an extra hour to do some research in the library. That wasn't really the truth, but a ruse to avoid everyone's finding out that Julie Peters, mama's little jewel, must be whisked away after school and locked up for safe-keeping. She turned to Laura and said, "Okay, I could use something to drink."

This was the second time Julie found herself succumbing to one of this exuberant girl's requests. Why? she asked herself. Probably because she was curious, not only about Laura but about herself. She wondered how she would interact with another girl in a situation so different from any she had known. Always before she had seen the young models she'd worked with through her mother's eyes—as competition. And they had seen her the same way, so there was no possibility of friendship.

Laura led the way to a small shop called Jack's Place, redolent with the strong smells of salami, pickles, and herring. As they settled themselves in a red plastic-covered booth toward the rear, Laura said, "A few of the kids come here when they're flush, but not too many. Jack charges outrageous prices just to keep them out. They're too noisy, he says. That's why I chose this place. It's easier to talk here."

Julie glanced around, grateful that the shop was uncrowded and the booth partitions high enough for at least a little privacy. As Laura ordered a Coke, Julie was about to ask the waitress for a diet soda when the thought struck her that she no longer had to watch her diet so religiously. "I'll have the same," she said.

As they waited for their drinks, a group of four high school girls took an empty booth across from them.

After the waitress had served them and left, Laura said, "I was going to tell you about the cause—at least, that's what Jeff and I call it. You see, my dad, when he was alive, and some of his friends started the Animal Rights Society. Dad felt that most people in this country have no idea of the senseless cruelty inflicted on animals, sometimes in the name of medical science and sometimes for other reasons which everyone thinks necessary but, too often, aren't. It's the job of the society to make people aware of that."

Julie had never given animals much thought. If anything, she'd always marveled that there were people in the world, undoubtedly like Laura and her father, who would put all kinds of energy into trying to save some obscure, threatened species.

Laura went on, "That's what I was doing when I organized the protest march—I was trying to make people aware of something I felt was wrong. And, I'm afraid, that's what Jeff was doing when he gave your name to the paper. He knew you would draw more attention than just a bunch of us nobodies."

You may have meant well, but you still could have given me a choice, Julie thought, but she said nothing, hoping to put the whole miserable experience behind her.

Laura changed the subject. "Talk about drawing attention—I have to tell you—those guys in the booth across from us"—she nodded toward the four girls whom Julie had noticed a short while ago—"they're from Kennedy High, and ever since they came in they've been gawking at you. They all know who you are. It's a wonder they're not over here asking for your autograph."

When Julie glanced over toward them, they quickly turned away and started tittering. She sighed. "You know, I've spent three days at Kennedy and no one has said a word to me—not *even* to ask for an autograph—except my teachers, you, and Mr. Webber. And he only wanted to let me know that I'd better not think of doing any more demonstrating."

"He didn't!" Laura sounded appalled.

"Yes, he did."

"Oh, I'm so sorry. I didn't mean to get you into anything like that. I can see his calling me on the carpet, because I organized everything, but you—"

"He talked to you too?"

Laura snorted, "You bet. He said he respected my beliefs as he would my religion but if I make any more trouble— watch out!"

"He told *me* I should be a better role model for all the young women in the country."

They stared at each other for a moment, then both burst out laughing. Somehow the whole experience seemed less important to Julie now and the session with Mr. Webber, funny. "He said," she imitated him, " 'I suppose you thought it was all a sort of lark.' "

Laura took up the imitation with " 'I certainly uphold all your First Amendment rights to protest, but do it again and I'll have your head.' "

Julie followed with " 'We're all entitled to one mistake.' "

That broke them up again. When their laughter finally died, Laura shook her head and said, "That guy is so oily I can't stand him."

"I know what you mean."

Laura changed the subject. "You know, you said that nobody's talked to you since you've been here except me— and I guess I wouldn't have if my mother hadn't sold you your house. That gave me an excuse. Everyone else is afraid of you."

Julie felt bewildered. "Afraid?"

"Well, maybe afraid isn't the right word. *Awe* is more like it. You're a celebrity to the rest of us and celebrities just aren't real flesh-and-blood people that you hold conversations with. I mean, celebrities don't sweat or get zits or other disgusting things like that."

"You mean no one will accept me unless I sprout pimples?"

"No, I didn't mean that. I just meant that to the kids at Kennedy, you're an unreal picture that stepped out of a magazine. They feel they wouldn't know what to say to you because, naturally, you wouldn't talk about the ordinary everyday stuff the rest of us do."

"But how can they feel that way when they don't even know me?"

"That's just the trouble. They *don't* know you. And they can't begin to imagine that you might be interested in knowing them."

"You make it sound so hopeless."

"Maybe not," Laura said. "I have an idea. If you want, I'll ask a few of the girls I like over to my house to meet you. We could do it this Sunday afternoon if that would be okay with you. My mother is usually out showing houses then, and Jeff works so we'll have the place to ourselves."

Julie hesitated, then finally said, "I guess it's worth a try."

"If you wouldn't mind, you could tell us something about

what it's like to have a modeling career. We're all dying to know what that kind of life is really like. Maybe you could even show us how to make up. That would be lot of fun."

As much as Julie felt she would like having a friend, she still had reservations. Was Laura really trying to help her, she asked herself, or was she simply using her as a star attraction to make herself look good? Then Julie chided herself for the never-ending suspicions that so often plagued her. Would she ever trust anyone? She said, shyly, "I'd be glad to tell them anything I know about the business. And I've got tons of makeup I could help them experiment with if you think they'd be interested."

"They'll be interested, believe me."

The waitress laid the check on their table, and Laura snatched it. "On me," she said.

"I owe you one," Julie said.

Laura laughed. "And don't think I'll let you forget it."

They got up to leave and Julie followed Laura to the cashier's desk. As Laura paid the bill, three young men entered the shop. One of them spotted Laura and said, "Hi, Laura, how y' doin'?"

Laura spun around, a surprised look on her face, and murmured, "Brian . . ."

Before she could say another word, he said, "Well, see you around." He gave a quick glance toward Julie, then shoved his staring buddies along toward the booths. Julie noticed that Laura, glancing after him, wore a disappointed look on her face. Now what was that all about? Julie wondered.

4

"How did you get started as a model, Julie?" Stephanie Behrens asked.

She was one of the four girls Laura had invited to her house that Sunday afternoon. They sat around a living room that Julie found much more inviting than her own, possibly because her mother was furnishing theirs in something Julie dubbed *Elegant Chic*. This room had a style of its own, with chairs and sofas all covered in slightly faded slipcovers, undoubtedly there to hide even greater wear beneath, yet the whole effect was one of comfort. You knew this was not a showplace but a home in which people lived.

The girls, Stephanie, Pam, Ann Marie, and Sara, acted as if they were very privileged indeed to be included in Laura's selection. All of which made Julie feel a little awkward and self-conscious. To answer Stephanie's question, she said, "It was my mother who started me. I was only eight then. She used to take me on go-sees."

Laura said, "What in the world are those?"

"They're just what the name suggests. You go see if people

who are looking for models want to use you. You take your book along, of course. That's a portfolio of your photographs. Or you go on auditions."

Pam, a mouse of a girl, too short to ever become a high-fashion model, said, "Oh, I'd be so nervous, doing something like that."

Julie nodded solemnly. "That's something you never get over—at least, I never did." She remembered how, in the beginning, she had always been so relieved when some other little girl got the job. Later, though, she'd felt guilty, knowing how she had disappointed her mother.

Ann Marie, a good ten pounds overweight, stared at Julie out of oversized designer glasses, admiration in her eyes. "I can't imagine someone like you ever feeling nervous."

"Oh, for Pete's sake," Laura exclaimed. "Julie's a human being too, you know. Of course she gets nervous once in a while, just like anybody. I'll bet even Princess Di gets nervous sometimes." The four stared at her with expressions that suggested she was out of her mind. Laura ignored them.

Stephanie, Julie noticed, loved to strike poses. She tossed a mane of dark, shiny hair back from her face, held her head at a regal angle, and said, "Do you think any of us could become models?"

That was not a question Julie was expecting. What could she say? If she was honest, they would hate her. She tried to answer by generalizing. "If you didn't work in New York you could never make it to the top. That's where all the important magazines and agencies are—the world-class photographers, too."

Stephanie persisted. "Well, assuming we did live in New York—would any of us be the right type?"

They all seemed to be leaning anxiously toward Julie. She

35

squirmed in her seat. "Well, there *are* standards. For instance, for high fashion, you have to be at least five foot seven."

"Whoops," Laura said, "that lets me out."

"Me too," Pam said, not sounding at all disappointed.

Stephanie scowled. "Even in heels I'd never make five seven."

Ann Marie shifted her plump bottom on the sofa and asked, "How much do you have to weigh?"

"Actually, the ideal model is five foot nine and one hundred ten pounds."

Ann Marie sighed wistfully. "That's really skinny." Her glance shot to Sara who, until now, had taken everything in and said nothing. All eyes followed Ann Marie's.

Laura said, "How tall are you, Sara?"

Sara, blond and pale, grinned. "I'm five ten and a half, but I weigh close to a hundred and thirty. So that lets me out."

"You could always diet," Pam said.

"No thanks." From a dish on the coffee table, Sara helped herself to a piece of Laura's homemade fudge. "I like to eat too well. Besides, I'm lazy. I can't see myself exercising a couple of hours a day and walking around with a book on my head. No, that's not the life for me."

"But, just think," Stephanie said, "men would fall at your feet."

Julie said, "I hate to disillusion you, but you wouldn't have time for men."

"No men!" they exclaimed in unison.

Pam added, "If that's the case, I guess I'll just leave the modeling to somebody else."

The others agreed, and Julie felt relieved to find herself

off the hook. Then Stephanie turned to her and asked, "Does that mean you've never had a boyfriend?"

Julie, embarrassed, could feel all eyes on her. How could she tell them the truth? No, she had never had a real boyfriend. When she needed an escort, her agent, Morgan, arranged for some well-known teen singer or actor to accompany her. If none was available, she would line up some up-and-coming photographer or designer who was glad to be seen out rubbing elbows with the famous. There was always someone but no one who mattered. "I've just always been too busy," she said.

Sara said, "If you're not modeling, you shouldn't be too busy now."

Again Julie could feel all eyes on her. She couldn't bring herself to tell them that even today her parents kept a close watch on her. Especially her mother. Her father, although he tried to hide it, was always concerned about her movements, always afraid some harm would befall her, even in this quiet, conservative town.

The girls began discussing which boy at Kennedy High might be suitable for Julie. He had to be tall, of course. And good-looking.

"How about Kevin Ford?" Pam said. "He's really a hunk."

Laura sneered. "He may be on the football team, but he's got a brain the size of a pea. I asked him to demonstrate with us, and you'd think with a brother who's a biology major in college he'd have learned to care about animals, but you know what he said? He said, 'You gotta be kidding.' "

Sara said, "That figures. He's got one line for everything. You could say you think it's going to rain and Kevin would answer, 'You gotta be kidding.' Big conversationalist."

They all laughed; then Pam, the mouse, changed the subject, and said to Laura, "I just think it was so brave of you and Julie to demonstrate the way you did. I'd never have the nerve to do something like that."

Julie felt she was accepting accolades she didn't deserve. Her part in the affair had nothing to do with bravery. She opened her mouth to protest, then thought better of it. There was no point in again bringing up her reaction to that disturbing event.

"I just hope the whole thing did some good," Laura said, "but I doubt it."

Stephanie said, "Didn't you hear?" Then she caught herself. "Oh, I didn't mean to say anything, because it's not common knowledge."

"Come on, Steph, give," Sara said.

Stephanie was obviously bursting to tell. "You've got to promise not to say anything."

Everyone promised.

"Well, you know my father's on the school board. He says they wrote a formal letter to Mr. Davis, requesting that in the future he refrain from using live animals for slaughtering demonstrations. Dad says the board felt Kennedy didn't need that kind of publicity."

Laura said, "You gotta be kidding!"

Everyone laughed, even Julie. Laura said to her, "We must have really done some good, and a lot of the credit is owing to you—most of it, I'll bet."

Julie smiled self-consciously. Was Laura right? Had the use of *her* name and *her* picture made the difference?

She didn't have time to ponder the issue because Stephanie said, "Laura, you said Julie was going to show us how they make up models."

"How about it, Julie?" Laura said.

Julie smiled agreeably. She spent the rest of the afternoon applying makeup to five faces. If the first part of the get-together had felt strained to her, the rest was a real ice-breaker with much ooohing and aaahing and giggling. They all agreed that everyone looked marvelous, but Sara's new look was a complete transformation and, minus a few pounds, she could compete with the best high-fashion models. Julie had never felt more useful or more like a true expert.

Finally, Sara glanced at her watch and exclaimed, "Wow, it's nearly time for dinner. I didn't realize it was getting so late."

No one realized, it seemed. They said their good-byes with enthusiastic, if vague, suggestions for getting together again and piled into Sara's dad's car, borrowed for the occasion. Julie and Laura waved them off, then went back inside the house.

"I'd better call my dad," Julie said. "He dropped me off and told me to let him know when I was ready for him to pick me up."

"You don't drive?" Laura asked.

Something about Laura's tone made Julie feel like a backward child. "Well, no. I've never learned. You see, I never needed a car in New York. There were always cabs. My father had one though—a Mercedes. He shipped it out here when we moved. Mostly my mother's using it now. She chauffeurs both of us around."

"Won't she let you borrow it?"

"I don't drive—remember?"

"Can't she teach you?"

"Not really. She's too nervous. Besides, she hasn't driven in years. She's just getting used to it again."

"What about your father?"

"He doesn't have enough free time." Until now, the problem of Julie's learning to drive had never even come up. She asked herself what her mother and father would say if she broached the subject. Certainly they would not welcome the idea. After all, they'd reason, if she could drive, she'd want her own car. If she had her own car, she'd go tooling around by herself, unprotected and vulnerable to all kinds of unimaginable dangers.

Laura said, "I wish I could offer to teach you, but I don't very often have the use of a car. Now and then I borrow Mom's or Jeff's for short runs, but I don't get to drive enough to feel like a really capable teacher. Not only that, I don't have the kind of patience it takes."

Maybe I really don't want to learn anyhow, Julie thought; then Dr. Almquist's words about the need to make decisions flashed through her mind. "They needn't be big decisions . . . start small. Maybe you'd like to learn how to roller-skate or take an art class or wear funky clothes—whatever. When the urge hits you, go with it. And don't let anyone talk you out of it!" He hadn't mentioned learning how to drive, but it was that kind of thing he'd meant.

"I suppose it's really not that much of a problem," Laura said. "Stephanie used a driver training school. She had her license in no time. You could always do that. Or you could sign up for driver training in school."

Maybe Laura thought it wasn't much of a problem, but Julie knew better. An instructor from a driving school would have to pick her up at home. And with driver training, her parents would probably have to sign something. Either way, her mother would find out and, somehow, talk her out of it. *Wait,* her mother would say. She'd use Julie's breakdown as a reason. *Wait until you feel more stable.* And Julie knew she never would feel more stable until she learned how to function independently. Suddenly the idea of learning to drive, maybe even owning her own car, loomed as an important symbol of that independence.

Julie said, "I really would like to learn how to drive, but I'd rather not go to a driving school or take driver training right now. I don't want my parents to find out." She couldn't bring herself to tell Laura why. "I—I'd like to surprise them. If I could just find someone with a car who'd take the time to teach me, I'd be glad to pay whatever the driving schools charge."

Laura's eyes lit up. "That's a great idea. Maybe my boyfriend, Brian, could—" She broke off. "Stupid me, I almost forgot. We had a falling out not long ago. I don't even think he's my boyfriend anymore."

Brian. The boy in the deli. So that was what that was all about, Julie thought.

Laura said, "Come to think of it, he wouldn't be any good anyhow. He's just as impatient as I am. I have another thought, though. A lot of the guys at the university are always looking to earn money. I'll bet Jeff could line up someone."

"I'd have to make some special kind of arrangement though, so that no one will find out."

"No problem. You can say you're studying with me. We'll find someone who'll pick you up and bring you back here."

"What if one of my parents wants to get in touch with me while I'm gone?"

"Simple. We'll turn on my mother's answering machine." Laura smiled mischievously. "I have a devious mind."

Julie laughed. "You've thought of everything." This was the first secret she had ever considered keeping from her parents. She could see herself, a free spirit, with her own

41

wheels going and coming as she pleased, a mature adult rather than a dependent child. "Oh, I just hope it works," she said.

"Don't worry, it will."

"How can I find out how much it will cost?" Julie wanted to be sure her spending money would take care of it. Checks could give away the plan.

"I'll call Stephanie tonight and find out what she paid the driving school, then I'll call you to be sure the price is okay before I set up anything. How does that sound?"

It sounded like just about the greatest adventure of her life.

5

On the drive home from the university that afternoon, Jeff had second thoughts about committing himself to teaching Julie to drive. What had possessed him anyhow? Sure, she was going to pay top dollar. And sure, he needed the money. But was it worth putting up with some prima donna celebrity?

Maybe she'd back out, though. Maybe when she discovered that he was to be her driving instructor she'd have second thoughts too. Laura had said, "I don't think she'll go for it, Jeff. She was really miffed about how you called the paper."

"So tell her it's strictly business. She wants to learn to drive, and I want the money. We don't have to like each other."

Laura had hesitated. "I just don't know." She'd thought it over for a couple of minutes, then said, "I tell you what— I'll say you've lined up some guy from school. Then when you show up instead, you can say that he couldn't make it, but you'll be glad to take the job if it's okay with her. She can always say no if she really wants to."

Now that the moment was upon him, Jeff felt uncomfortable with the thought of telling some phony story to foist himself off on her. He was a rotten liar anyhow.

As he pulled into the driveway, he spotted Laura and Julie standing outside, chatting, obviously waiting for the new driving instructor to show. He turned off the ignition, got out of the car, and made his way toward them.

Laura greeted him with a look of feigned surprise. "What are *you* doing here, Jeff?"

He refused to play the game. "I live here, remember?"

She made a great show of glancing up the street as if expecting someone to come tearing around the corner. "Where's the guy who's going to teach Julie to drive?"

She should have been an actress, he thought. "He had to back out at the last minute." Jeff gave a helpless shrug. "Sorry," Now that he was face to face with Ms. Famous Teenage Model, he decided that he was out of his depth. Let her find someone else. So she looked disappointed. So too bad.

When he offered nothing, Laura hopped in with, "I have a wonderful idea, Julie. Jeff can teach you. He's a great teacher. He taught me. Besides, he's always trying to earn extra money for school. How about it, Jeff?"

Julie, looking rattled, shook her head. "Oh, I don't think—" She broke off.

Laura said, "He really is a good teacher."

From the expression on Julie's face, Jeff could tell his services were unwelcome. Which was certainly all right with him. He had better things to do anyhow. "Can't you find some guy in your class who wants to earn money?" he asked Laura.

She looked mystified. "But I thought you—I mean, I thought you were always looking for extra jobs yourself."

Julie said, "That's all right, Laura. It doesn't matter."

Laura glared at Jeff. "Of course it matters. It was supposed to be all set up. We even went to all the trouble of getting a learner's permit."

"But it doesn't have to be today," Julie said.

Laura studied her for a moment. "You look relieved. That's bad. That's really bad. That means if you don't do it now, you never will. You'll get cold feet. I know I would."

"It's all right, Laura," Julie insisted. "Honestly. I'll find someone else. I'm sure your brother has other things to do."

She seemed anxious to back out, Jeff thought. Naturally she was still mad at him but maybe other things were bothering her too. Maybe she found him too offensive to sit next to for an hour two or three times a week. Or maybe she assumed he'd make a pass at her. Fat chance. Feeling perverse now, he said, "It just happens that I don't have anything pressing to do this afternoon. We'll give it a try. Come on."

"Great!" Laura said and, without giving Julie a chance to decline, grabbed her hand and pulled her along toward Jeff's Mustang.

Jeff almost felt sorry for the girl. She looked about as desperate as someone being kidnapped. He strode around to the passenger side of the car and opened the door. "You'd better sit here for now. We'll find a spot with less traffic, then you can take over."

"But—" she said weakly as Laura virtually pushed her inside.

Jeff headed for the driver's side and slid into the seat. "Don't worry. I won't start charging until you have the wheel." Might as well make it clear that this was a business arrangement, and that he expected pay for his services. He started the engine, and as he pulled out of the driveway, Laura waved them off shouting, "You'll be okay, Julie. Jeff's a terrific teacher."

They drove in silence as Jeff headed for an area just outside town called Morningside, a planned industrial park where the roads were wide and almost traffic-free at that hour of the day. This was the place he'd used to start Laura. He parked, turned off the ignition, got out, and went around to open the door for her.

"Here's where we change places," he said. When she sat for a moment, looking frozen, he added, "You'll have to go around, I'm afraid. You can't slide over very easily. The gearshift is in the way."

"Oh," she said vaguely and got out of the car.

Now he had a chance to look her over in a way he hadn't had time for during the demonstration. Although he was over six feet himself he decided she was too tall, too slender, and her manner too standoffish for his taste. He had to admit that she was nice-looking though, if you liked the type, but no one would have ever guessed that she was some high-priced model. That is, not until she walked around to the driver's seat, handling herself with the practiced grace of royalty. Princess Julie, no doubt.

As he took the seat beside her, she made no move to grasp the steering wheel or to assume a driver's position. Instead, she glanced at him questioningly, apparently awaiting instruction. He wondered if she *ever* took the initiative. "Have you had any driving experience at all?" he asked.

"No—not any."

"I hope you weren't expecting to learn on a car with automatic transmission." He could tell from her expression that she had never given the matter any thought. She obviously had no idea what made a car run.

"I suppose a car with automatic transmission would be easier to learn on," she said.

Thank God for small mercies! She might not have known anything else, but at least she must have grasped the difference between manual and automatic transmission. "Yes, it would be easier. It'll take longer to learn the stick shift, but at least when you finally get your license, you'll be a better driver. It's up to you, though. If you don't want to try this, we can call it a day, and Laura can shop around for someone else to teach you." There! She couldn't say he hadn't given her every chance to change her mind.

She hesitated. At length she said, "I suppose I should give it a try."

He shrugged as if the whole thing were a matter of complete indifference to him. "Okay. Let's begin." He explained the relationship of the controls and, without the engine running, had her practice using the clutch and shifting gears. When he thought she had the idea, he said, "Now let's start the car. The only way to learn is to get out on the road."

She shot him a frightened glance. "I don't know how to start the car."

"Of course you don't. I haven't told you how yet. That's next." What a drag this was going to be, he thought. Laura had been all too ready to take the bull by the horns, but this one was going to need prodding every step of the way. "Don't

47

be afraid. There's no one on the road right now, and I'm right beside you to grab the wheel if you do something wrong."

If she did something wrong? During the next ten minutes or so she did *everything* wrong. She ground the gears, stalled the car, flooded the engine, had the thing bucking until he thought they were going to take off. *I'm sorry, I'm sorry,* she kept saying until he couldn't stand it anymore. He made her stop the car while he gave her a lecture. "Now, let's understand something. You're going to do things wrong until you get the feel of what you're doing. You must have apologized at least fifteen times now. Let's let that cover all future mistakes. Okay?" If he sounded superior, he didn't care. She was probably used to everyone's kowtowing to her anyhow.

He couldn't read her expression as she said, "I'll try to remember."

She started again, and the car shot out as if it had a mind of its own. "Hit the brake," he yelled, not even bothering to try to sound calm.

She lifted her foot from the gas as if she'd been stung, aimed for the brake, missed, and jammed down on the gas again. With the engine revving hysterically, the car tore forward, throwing Jeff back in his seat and off balance. He quickly recovered and reached over to turn off the ignition. As they coasted to a stop, he silently thanked whatever gods were smiling on them for the empty street.

"I'm sorry, I'm sorry," she said.

His well-meaning lecture had disappeared on the wind. "No harm done," he muttered.

"Maybe I should wait until I find someone with automatic transmission."

That's for sure, he thought. Well, if she was asking for his opinion, he wasn't about to oblige. Undoubtedly, all her life things had come easy for her. So let her struggle now. It would teach her a little something about life. He ignored her words and said, "Start the car again. We'll take everything a step at a time. Keep your speed under thirty miles an hour. This road goes around the tract. When you've circled it a couple of times, we'll concentrate on right turns. That will be enough for today."

She managed the gears without incident this time and timidly made her way around the complex. He snapped orders at her. *Keep your hands at the top of the wheel. Ease out the clutch. A little more gas. Don't grind the gears.* He knew he was being hard on her, but he told himself that that was exactly what she needed. Wouldn't hurt her to work for something for once.

Now and then an odd car appeared in the area, someone going to or coming from one of the businesses there. Each of them gave the Mustang a wide berth. Apparently they were used to student drivers using their road.

After she seemed a little easier with driving in third gear, he had her concentrate on right turns, all of which she executed with a beginner's awkwardness. He allowed her no quarter, barking out more and more orders. *You're turning too wide. Now you're too close to the curb. Let the wheel slide back by itself. Too much gas. Too little gas.* Each turn was worse than the last and, with each, his criticism increased.

Finally the hour was up, and he had her pull over to the side of the road and park. "You just don't seem to be getting the feel of it," he said. "You're not doing what I tell you to do. You were much too wide on that last turn, you forgot to brake, and you were pouring in gas. I don't know how you're ever going—" He broke off when he realized that all the time he was talking she was paying no attention but muttering something under her breath.

"I can't do it, I can't do it. I'll never be able to do it," he heard her say, hardly above a whisper. Then she did something that completely threw him. She made a choking noise that he realized was an attempt to stifle a sob. In the next instant, tears rolled down her cheeks. As she tried to wipe them away, she said, "I'm sorry, I'm sorry . . ."

He forgot all about who she was. She was merely a sensitive girl whose self-assurance (and he rather doubted that she'd had all that much to start with) he had all but destroyed. He felt like a heel, knowing very well that he had been deliberately trying to give her a bad time. In teaching driving, you never made pupils spend too long in repeating maneuvers that were difficult for them, because they soon tired, tensed, and lost confidence. The idea was to help them relax. That was the only way to learn. He glanced over to her, at a loss to know how to comfort her. "Hey, you weren't that bad. This is only your first day. You should have seen some of the dumb stunts I pulled when I started."

She shook her head, a defeated expression on her face. "I'll never be able to do it—never."

"Sure you will. It'll get easier each time—you'll see. Besides, it's really my fault if you're all worn out. I've been working you much too hard for your first time. It's a miracle that you've stood up as well as you have."

She wiped the tears off her cheeks and gave a small smile. "I wouldn't call this standing up very well."

"Blame me." She was so different from what he imagined she would be like, so much more vulnerable! "The next time everything will go a lot better."

50

She hesitated. "I'm not sure there should be a next time."

"You're not giving up after only one try, I hope. Besides, you're starting to do well, coordinating the clutch and gear. That's usually the hardest thing for a beginner."

She looked at him doubtfully. "Do you really think so?"

"I sure do. You're going to be fine. Don't be so hard on yourself. Learning to drive, like anything else, takes time. You're off to a good start."

"You didn't seem to think so a little while ago."

He said sheepishly, "My bark is worse than my bite. No kidding, you're really doing okay."

She shrugged. "If you say so."

"The sooner we go out again, the better. We have to build your confidence. Can you make it tomorrow afternoon?"

"If you're willing, I am."

"Good. We'll make it the same time. Now we'd better head for home. Today I'll drive, but tomorrow you can do it."

"Ugh!"

He laughed. "You'll surprise yourself." This was the treatment he should have been giving her all along. From now on he vowed he'd act differently.

They changed seats and Jeff drove home. When he pulled into his driveway, Laura came running out of the house and over to the car. She seemed full of her usual exuberance with a touch of something else that hadn't been there earlier. As Julie and Jeff got out of the Mustang, she asked, "How did it go?"

"Oh, I'm a dunce," Julie said.

Laura said, "So was I." Then she turned to Jeff. "The phone was busy while you were gone. The ARS called. They're demonstrating Saturday in front of I. Magnin because there'll be a fur sale going on. They want both of us to make it. Will you be able to?"

"Yes, I think so."

"And guess what!" Without waiting for an answer, Laura said, "Brian called, and we made up. And not only that, I'm trying to talk him into demonstrating with us. I think I can do it, because you know how he hates missing excitement."

"I wish you luck," Jeff said, not too glad to receive that piece of news. Now he'd probably have to follow through with the talk his mother wanted him to give Laura about seeing Brian too much. He glanced over to Julie and saw that she was busily engaged in looking through her handbag for something. Suddenly the thought occurred to him that she was pretending to be too involved to hear the talk of the upcoming demonstration, undoubtedly worried that they might ask her to participate.

Laura must have sensed the same thing, because she said, "Don't worry, Julie, I'm not going to drag you into it this time."

Jeff saw Julie's face redden. The memory of how he had sicced reporters on her such a short time ago came rushing back, making him feel ashamed. She was obviously a very sensitive person.

6

"There'll be signs for each of you. It's all arranged for Saturday's demonstration," Laura said to Stephanie, Pam, Ann Marie, and Sara as they lunched with Julie in the school cafeteria.

Julie's mind was in two places. A part of her kept thinking about yesterday's driving lesson. Maybe she *had* acted stupidly, but who did Jeff think he was anyhow? God? He'd certainly behaved that way. Probably he felt superior just because he was a college student. She dreaded facing her next session with him even though he had seemed more sympathetic toward the end.

Another part of her mind was trying to take in what the girls were talking about. Laura had convinced her that they were dying to socialize with her. "They said they thought you were a regular guy," Laura had said. "That happens to be a real compliment from this bunch. Of course I have to admit they don't mind being seen with somebody as famous as you either."

Julie, resentful that her worth always seemed to be measured by her celebrity status, said, "I'm not sure I like that."

"Well, you should." Laura sounded like a great authority on such matters. "They feel that if somebody special notices them and wants to be friends with them, then that makes *them* special too. That's not so bad, is it?"

Somebody special. Julie wondered how she could have spent so many years as a model in the public eye without ever once thinking of herself as somebody special. "When you put it that way, no, it doesn't sound bad at all." Then why do I still feel like a fifth wheel with this group? she asked herself.

Stephanie said, "I don't know, Laura. I'm not sure I'm not being a hypocrite, demonstrating about furs when my mother owns a mink coat."

"That's not important," Laura said. "Her generation didn't know any better, but *we* do. The important thing is that we never wear furs and that we educate people about the suffering that's involved just to feed somebody's vanity."

Julie thought of the beautiful beaver coat she had in storage in New York, along with the sable with perfectly matched skins that belonged to her mother. Should she feel apologetic or guilty because they both owned something that women all over the world prized?

Pam said to her, "Laura's going with Brian on Saturday, but the rest of us are going in Stephanie's car. There's room for you if you want to come with us, Julie."

Julie, flustered, glanced over to Laura, who said quickly, "Julie can't make it that day."

All eyes fastened on Julie as though waiting for an explanation, probably because she'd been a part of the lamb protest. Instead of obliging them, she asked, "Why didn't any of you demonstrate with Laura over the slaughtering in class?"

"We were afraid," Pam said.

Sara, of the boyish good looks, smiled mischievously. "You mean we were chicken. We were all scared it would go against us on our school records."

"You and Laura were the only brave ones," Ann Marie said.

Not I, Julie thought. I was just too stupid to know better. "Is this the first time you've gone to one of these things?"

Sara chuckled. "Heck, no. Laura makes sure we show at every animal rights demonstration within a hundred miles of here."

"It's fun," Pam said. When Laura gave her a disgusted look, she added, "Well, it *is* fun, even if it is for a worthy cause."

In between bites of her sandwich, Sara said, "You can't be around Laura for any length of time without getting brainwashed."

Laura said indignantly, "I wouldn't call learning the truth brainwashing."

"I'm kidding, I'm kidding," Sara said.

Plump Ann Marie nibbled from a dish of wilted-looking greens and eyed the fat chocolate-covered cupcake that sat in front of Pam. "Actually," she said, "we've learned a lot from Laura—things that people just don't seem to know about all this stuff."

Pam's eyes suddenly held the gleam of a zealot. "It's true," she said to Julie. "Did you know they still use steel-jaw leghold traps to catch wild animals?"

Julie, not wanting to display her ignorance, merely shook her head.

"Well, they do. They catch fifteen to twenty-five million animals that way every year. They set up the traps with bait, and when the animals step into them, these things clamp down on their legs and hold them there, sometimes for weeks."

Sara shuddered as she went on from where Pam left off. "Some animals die of starvation, and some chew off their own legs to get free. If trappers get to them before they're dead, lots of times those guys won't waste bullets. They just bludgeon the poor creatures to death. Right, Laura?"

Laura nodded solemnly. "It really makes me sick to think that twenty to sixty animals have to die—and die brutally—for every fur coat that's sold. And trapping is only a small part of the whole thing. Fur farming is just as bad."

She went on to tell Julie about the various methods used in killing farmed animals with chloroform or cyanide. And then there was strychnine, a poison that made the animal's muscles contract in painful cramps that resulted in suffocation.

When she finished, Pam said, "Some breeders even wring the animals' necks. Imagine! Others drug them, then electrocute them, only sometimes the electrocution doesn't work, even though the drug makes the animals *look* dead. So they get skinned alive."

Ann Marie regarded Pam through her large glasses and said, "For someone who looks like a fragile size five, you sure enjoy dishing out the gore."

"But it's true," Pam said primly and started on her cupcake.

Stephanie glanced over to Ann Marie. "Pam knows you're trying to diet. She thought she'd help out."

Ann Marie's eyes were glued to Pam's chocolate cupcake. "Unfortunately, with me, it works the opposite way. Things that make other people lose their appetites make me want to eat all the more. I wonder if there's time to get some dessert."

Stephanie pushed a piece of Sara Lee cake, still in its wrapper, over to Ann Marie. "Here, take mine. I'm one of those 'other people.' "

Laura said, "Well, it *should* make you upset—all of you." She gave Julie a meaningful glance.

Julie stared down into her half-eaten plate of tuna salad, sure the others could look into her eyes and see the beaver coat and her mother's sable, and all the beautiful furs—minks, chinchillas, nutrias, foxes, more than she could remember—that she had modeled in her lifetime. She felt as if the whole conversation had been directed at her, because she was the only one of them not demonstrating.

But everyone wore furs. At least everyone she had known in the East. Were Californians different? Or was it merely that furs in this climate were, as Morgan would put it, *de trop*? Surely Laura was a fanatic who had indeed brainwashed her friends, as they themselves claimed. Why then did they all make her feel so guilty?

On Saturday morning Julie stared out the family-room window at the oversized swimming pool, as yet unused because the weather was still too chilly. The blue water glittered invitingly in the sunlight. She wondered if there would ever come a day when she would have the nerve to invite people in to swim and visit and just have fun.

She thought of her last driving lesson and felt even worse. At least she hadn't cried this time, and Jeff had behaved with more patience although, somehow, she felt he was merely suffering her. From that first moment in his car she'd sensed

57

that he didn't like her. Or maybe *like* wasn't the right word. *Approve* was probably more like it.

Why? she wondered. Because I'm a weak-kneed dunce when it comes to handling a machine? That hardly seemed a solid reason. Or was that only a part of it? Maybe he expected someone with her background to be confident, poised, and outgoing—which she was not. Whatever the reason, why should she even care *what* he thought? After all, she was paying him for his time. She should be the one in the "driver's seat"—to make a very bad pun. At least he had let her drive back to his house this time, so she must have improved that much.

When all was said and done, the only important thing was that she prove to herself that she could master this thing and get a driver's license.

Her father's voice came from the kitchen. "Julie, what time did your mother say she'd be home?"

Julie called back to him. "She wasn't sure. Early after-noon, she thought. When she finishes with the decorator, she said she'd have some lunch downtown and do some shopping."

A moment later Harrison Peters strode into the family room, a cup of coffee in hand, and settled himself in an easy chair. Even in a casual cotton sweater and jeans, Julie thought, he still looked distinguished. "That means we'll have to get our own lunch." He grinned like a schoolboy playing hooky. "What shall we have? Hot cakes swimming in maple syrup? Belgian waffles with raspberries and ice cream? My famous cheese omelet, smothered in sauce Juliette?"

She couldn't help smiling. They played this game when her mother was not around, whippng up batches of rich, high-caloried food, forbidden until now because Julie had to keep her almost too-slender model's figure.

58

Since they'd come to Santa Delores, her parents had been trying to line up a housekeeper-cook but, so far, had found no one who suited. In the meantime, they were getting by with Julie's mother's spartan fare. For Julie, there was always one extra commandment: *Thou shalt not gain weight!* Right now though, food was the last thing on her mind. She said, "Let's wait until lunchtime to decide what we feel like."

Amusement glinted in his eyes. "With serious decisions like these, I believe in planning ahead. After all, I might have to go to the store. Your mother isn't likely to keep something like ice cream in the house."

They exchanged the smiles of conspirators. Julie said, "Then let's have your omelet. You won't have to go out for that."

He bowed his head in mock chivalry. "Your wish is my command, you foxy lady."

He could always raise her spirits, she thought.

He sipped his coffee, then said, "I thought you might be off with some of those new friends of yours today."

Julie settled on the divan facing him. "They're all demonstrating."

His eyebrows shot up. "You mean they still have that thing going about the lamb?"

"Oh, no. That was just that one day. They're demonstrating in front of I. Magnin because of the fur sale."

"They're what?"

Julie told him all about their conversation in the cafeteria. "They made it sound so awful—about what people do to animals just to make fur coats."

"They'd do better demonstrating for one of the causes about man's inhumanity to man," he said, stroking his dark beard the way he always did when he was being thoughtful. "You know, since time began, one species has always used

59

another in any way it wished or could, just as one animal has always been food for another. That's the way the world is. A bunch of well-meaning young people will never change that."

"I suppose not," Julie said wistfully.

"Do I detect a note of regret? Are you sorry you're not out there keeping your friends company?"

"Oh, no. How could I do that when I've worn furs myself?"

"But I'll bet you still feel as though you're missing all the excitement."

"I don't think that's it—exactly. I mean, I never thought about animals like that before. I've modeled furs, and they were just something beautiful to wear, not living creatures that had to suffer pain and die because someone wanted them on their backs. I don't even understand *why* I never gave it any thought before."

"Most of us feel we have enough human concerns without taking on those of the whole animal kingdom."

Julie could tell that he was finished with the subject, that what they were going to have for lunch really interested him more. "Maybe I *should* have demonstrated with them," she said, more to herself than to him.

His eyes narrowed. "Remember, Julie, you didn't like it before when they cashed in on your name. There's no guarantee you wouldn't be put in the same position again. Just be very sure that that's what you really want before you get involved."

Of course her father was right. What was she even thinking of? His words brought back the memory of the previous experience—the attacking reporters, her own panic, the newspaper accounts. . . . No, she was well out of it all.

Later that afternoon when her mother returned loaded down with purchases for the house, Julie was even more relieved that she'd had the good sense to forgo the demonstration.

Her mother said, "I don't know what we've got ourselves into, moving to a town this provincial. A bunch of idiots were out in front of I. Magnin, making a big hullabaloo about fur coats. I can't even imagine what kind of people would do something like that."

Julie, a note of defiance in her voice, said, "People like Laura Ryder."

"The realtor's daughter? The one you've been spending so much time with lately?"

"Yes."

Her mother pondered the information for a moment, then said, "Maybe you shouldn't see so much of that girl. I mean, you never can tell about fanatics. They can be very unstable. I'm just surprised she didn't rope you into this sideshow the way she did in that school thing."

"Oh, Mother, she's not a fanatic! She's just doing something she believes in. And I'm a big girl now. I know how to say no."

"Well, you didn't the last time. And fanatic or not, after that little episode at school, I certainly wouldn't trust her."

Julie wanted to remind her mother that she'd relished "that little episode at school" for the publicity it had brought. This time the demonstration must have struck too close to home. After all, who wants to be criticized for owning a beautiful coat made of perfectly matched sable skins.

You are a hypocrite, Mother, Julie thought.

7

The aroma of morning coffee filled the kitchen. Noreen Ryder, dressed for a busy Monday working day, bustled around, putting breakfast dishes in the dishwasher and wiping the tile counter, as Jeff finished cereal and toast.

"Where are our new pets this morning?" she asked.

"Probably asleep. They spent the night in Laura's room. You know how she loves cats."

"I know. I really didn't want any pets right now—we're all so busy—but, under the circumstances, I just couldn't refuse to take the poor things when Cal asked."

Calvin Wallace, the Ford dealer in Santa Delores, and now managing director of the Animal Rights Society, had worked with Jeff's father when he was alive. Together they'd found many a home for an ill-used pet. "We should be able to manage," Jeff said. "Cats don't mind spending time alone, the way dogs do."

"I suppose not," she said, then turned to another subject. "I heard Laura stirring, but I'm afraid I'm going to have to run before she comes downstairs. I have an early appointment today. How do I look?" In a new dove-gray suit with a white silk blouse, both severely tailored, she struck a pose for him.

"Nice," he said.

She chuckled. "This is my power suit. I'm showing some acreage to a really sharp contractor, and I want to look as though I know what I'm talking about. Gray is supposed to instill confidence, you know. Do you think I should wear a colorful scarf to soften the effect?"

He grinned. "Not if power is your game."

She smiled. "Jeff, I've been meaning to say this since the demonstration last Saturday. You did a fine job. Your dad would have been proud of you."

Jeff wasn't sure he deserved the praise. "We'll never know whether or not we did any good, I'm afraid."

"Good! I'd say getting on the channel four news was better than good."

Jeff shrugged. "Well, Laura's friends seemed to enjoy themselves anyhow. Especially Brian. He spent all his time making up phrases everybody could chant." Jeff still suspected Brian's only interest was the excitement—and Laura—rather than the cause.

"Oh, yes, speaking of Brian—when Laura comes down, you'd better talk to her about seeing so much of him. Ever since they patched up their squabble, it's been almost an every night thing."

The feeling of resentment that bothered him so much lately washed over him again. "I think it would be better if *you* talked to her, Mom."

"Oh, Jeff, you know she doesn't pay any attention to anything I say. The only person Laura ever listened to was your dad."

"Then I don't know why you think she'd listen to me."

"She respects what you think, Jeff. Besides, you have a way of talking to her that doesn't get her back up—just like your father."

"I wish you wouldn't keep saying that, Mom, because it's not true." Jeff couldn't imagine why his mother always insisted he was "just like" his father. Except for holding the same values, and their mutual concern for animals, he was very different. What's more, he couldn't understand where she got the idea that Laura would heed his sage words of advice. Fat chance.

"Jeff, just talk to her—okay?"

He sighed. "Okay."

"Now I've really got to run." She started to leave, then turned back, a big smile on her face. "Tonight when we have more time, I think the three of us should talk about taking a vacation this summer."

Jeff stared at her in disbelief. She must have known he hoped to return to the same law office in San Francisco where he'd clerked last year. "But, Mom—"

She stopped him. "I know what you're going to say, and you're wrong. We *can* afford it this year. Besides, we haven't had a real vacation since your father died. It's time we did."

"But, Mom—"

Again she stopped him. "I don't have time to talk about it now, but just be thinking about where we should go. We'll have one of our powwows tonight," she said, and was off before he could remind her of his intentions. Surely she'd simply forgotten all about San Francisco and about how much he could use the money toward his school expenses next year. He hated the thought of throwing cold water on her vacation plans, but he would simply have to remind her tonight.

As he got up and rinsed off his dishes to put them in the dishwasher, Laura bounced into the kitchen, looking fresh and ready to attack the day. As she bent over the coffeepot on the stove and inhaled deeply, he caught a whiff of scent that blended unhappily with the odor of coffee. She turned off the gas and said, "Coffee just never tastes as good as it smells."

Jeff, feeling testy after the conversation with his mother, decided that Laura was all too fond of greeting the day with that piece of wisdom. He offered no comment. Instead, he said, "How are the cats doing?"

"One of them is sleeping on my bed. The other is hiding in my closet."

"Will they be okay there all day?"

"Of course. I left water and dry food and a sandbox. If they want to they can wander around the house, but somehow I don't think they will. They're real scaredies, both of them." She took a container of orange juice from the refrigerator and filled a glass that sat waiting for her on the kitchen table.

"Aren't you going to have anything else?" Jeff asked.

"I'm not hungry. Besides, Brian's driving me to school. I won't have time. He should be here any minute."

Brian. No wonder she had doused herself in perfume. The name reminded him of his mother's words. "Laura, Mom wanted me to tell you that she thinks you're seeing too much of Brian. Why don't you ease off for a while. After all, this *is* your senior year. You could use the time better for study."

Laura stared at him, disbelief in her eyes. "What do you

65

think we've been doing? And right here in plain sight too."

"I know. But you know how Mom is. She worries about things like that. And right now, trying to earn a living in what amounts to a new career for her, she doesn't need *you* to worry about too."

She rolled her eyes. "Oh, man, do you realize how you sound?"

He shifted uncomfortably on his chair but said nothing.

She sat down at the table across from him. "You know, Jeff, how much I see of Brian is none of your business."

"Maybe not, but it *is* Mom's business."

"So let *her* tell me. Lately, you've been sounding more like my father than my brother. And I don't mind telling you that I don't like it one bit."

"Laura, I know. I don't mean to come on so heavy, but Mom doesn't have Dad to rely on anymore. She needs somebody to help her the way *he* used to. It seems to me that the least we can both do is try to make things easier for her."

She regarded him thoughtfully. "You know something, Jeff? I'm not sure that helping her the way Dad used to doesn't just make things harder for her."

"You've lost me."

"I know you think I'm pretty ditsy and a few other things, but one thing I'm not is stupid about what's going on inside people."

"What do you mean?"

"I mean, I think Mom needs some friends her own age. Haven't you noticed that no matter what she wants to do or where she wants to go, she always asks one of us to go with her?"

"And you always say no."

"Well, lots of times I have other things I want to do. And

sometimes I just want to do things with people my own age. But you *always* say yes."

"What else *can* I say when you refuse to go with her?"

"What else you can say is no."

"But she doesn't have anyone else to do things with."

"And she never will if we keep doing everything with her."

Laura's assessment of the situation touched a nerve. In many respects she was right. But it was easy for her to go her own way, knowing that he was there for their mother to rely on. If they both said no at the same time, he wondered if she would feel differently. Could she stand the guilt of knowing she was denying her mother a little pleasure after so many months of sadness? He might have pursued the subject, but a horn sounded outside, and Laura sprang to her feet, saying, "There's Brian. I've got to run."

She practically flew out of the house. He didn't even have a chance to ask her what she intended to do about seeing so much of Brian.

Brian seemed very personable, Julie thought, as he drove her and Laura to the Ryder home after school that afternoon. With sandy nondescript hair and average height, he was saved from passing for ordinary by brown eyes that gleamed with humor and deep dimples that, when he smiled, gave him the look of someone plotting good-humored mischief.

As he pulled into the Ryders' driveway, he glanced over to Laura, who sat next to him, and said, "I guess I won't be seeing you tonight then," sounding as if he were merely affirming some previous agreement.

Laura shook her head. "No. My mother is of the opinion that you're a bad influence on me."

Brian rolled his eyes. "That what *she* thinks." He grinned

67

and his dimples came into play. "She should talk to *my* mother."

"Never mind," Laura said, "I know how to fix 'em both. We'll make them quiz us every night on our homework."

Brian grinned. "What a great idea. That'll really drive them crazy."

"We'll make it so tough on them they won't be able to wait to set aside their scruples."

Brian gave her an affectionate poke with his elbow. "You know something? You're a nut."

Laura said, "You know something else? It takes one to know one." She gave him a quick peck on the lips and, laughing, followed Julie out of the car.

"Pick you up in the morning, same time," Brian said, then as an afterthought added, "Hey, Julie—this is a belated welcome to Santa Delores. You know, you could really put this place on the map."

Julie smiled. She knew he meant the words as a compliment, but she had no desire to put Santa Delores or any place else on "the map." "Thanks."

As they headed for the house, Laura said, "Jeff told me he'd be a tad late this afternoon, so let's wait inside."

"Fine with me. I'm never that anxious to get behind the wheel."

"What did you think of Brian?" Laura asked.

"He seems nice."

"He is—sometimes. Other times I could kill him. But, on the whole, we're pretty well matched. Both crazy."

Curious, because she couldn't imagine herself in a similar relationship, Julie said, "You seem to be so easy with each other."

"We should be. I've known him since middle school, and

68

we've gone steady, off and on, since we were juniors. My mother says we see too much of each other. I suspect she thinks we're into sex. She needn't worry though. Brian and I came to an understanding about that subject ages ago."

"Understanding?" Julie said stupidly. Sex was a commodity the modeling business sold blatantly, yet, in her case, it was only something about which she'd read but knew nothing of firsthand.

"Oh, yes. Brian knows exactly how I feel. Sure, I may be seventeen, but I'm still not ready for all the responsibility that goes with sex. After all, I'm the one who could get pregnant—not Brian. And I've just got too much living to do before I go that route."

Could you do that? Julie wondered. Simply say, No, I'm not ready? From everything she'd read, she had the impression that going steady always meant having sex. How strong-minded Laura must be. Because Julie didn't want to appear as ignorant as she was, she said, "I'm with you."

Laura shrugged, looking as if she had dismissed the subject as being of no consequence, and took out her key. As she turned it in the lock, a yowling set up from inside the house. "That's Jenny, telling me off for leaving her alone too long," Laura said, and opened the door to the highly vocal greeting of a small, long-haired tabby with dark coloring.

"I didn't know you had a cat," Julie said.

"We didn't until a couple of days ago. Now we have two. A friend of ours had to find homes for them, and we were fair game because, at the moment, we were petless."

As they stepped inside the entry hall, Laura quickly closed the door. "I haven't let her out yet. I felt she should get used to us and the house before she faces the big out-of-doors."

69

The cat rubbed against Laura's legs but when Julie reached down to stroke it, the animal shrank away. "I guess she doesn't like me," Julie said.

"Oh, it isn't that. She just hasn't learned to trust people yet."

"Oh? Why not?"

Laura strode into the living room and tossed her book bag on the sofa. As Julie followed, without facing her, Laura said, "No reason. Cats are like that—scared until they're used to you. You should see the one upstairs. She spent the first night hiding in my closet—wouldn't come out until the next day. And then she'd run back in if you as much as said boo. She still won't come downstairs yet."

"I had no idea cats were that timid."

Still avoiding Julie's eyes, Laura said, "Not all of them are."

Julie had the strange impression that there was more to be said on the subject, but, for some reason, Laura wasn't talking. "I really don't know anything about cats. I never had one of my own." She hoped the words would encourage Laura to share with her whatever it was she was keeping to herself.

Instead, Laura exclaimed, "You never had a cat?"

Laura's expression made Julie feel sadly wanting. "No."

"A dog?"

Julie shook her head. "My mother always said that New York was not the place for pets."

A crafty gleam deepened the blue of Laura's eyes. "You're not in New York anymore . . ."

Julie was so accustomed to a life without pets that the thought of owning one now that she was living in Santa Delores had never crossed her mind. "Like most kids, I

70

always thought I wanted a dog, but it wouldn't be fair to get one when I plan to go away to college next year."

"Oh, you're so right," Laura said agreeably. "Dogs need a lot of attention. On the other hand, cats aren't like that at all. They're independent. They can be content just living in a big house like yours. In fact, with the wonderful grounds around your place, it absolutely cries for cats."

Julie hesitated. She knew very well where Laura was heading but she wasn't quite sure how she felt about taking on the responsibility of owning a pet. "I don't know. My mother isn't big for pets—at least not dogs. I don't know how she'd feel about a cat." Julie thought of her dad and of all the stories he used to tell about the cats and dogs his family had owned when he was growing up. Certainly *he* wouldn't mind one around the house. She said absently, "My dad's an animal person though."

As soon as the words were spoken, Julie was sorry. Laura immediately pounced. "That settles it! I'm going to give you your pick of one of these guys—or should I say girls?— they're both females."

"Oh, I don't know—" Julie began, thinking again of her mother.

"Believe me, I wouldn't give either one of them to just anybody, but you're special. After all, you've never had a pet, and I know you'd treat one well."

"Of course I would, but I really don't think—"

"I'll even throw in a cat box with some litter and some food to get you started."

Laura was certainly persistent, and her offer was growing more tempting to Julie. Still she had reservations. "I just don't know whether I could sell my mother on the idea."

Laura, who always seemed to be on top of every situation,

said, "I have the perfect solution. Take the cat home and see how it works out. If it doesn't, we'll take her back." She grabbed Julie's hand and pulled her along toward the stairs. "Come on. We'll find the other one—then you can choose."

Laura had to fish "the other one" out from under her bed. The cat, white with an odd assortment of orange, gray, and black spots, cowered in her arms, head hidden in the folds of her sweater. "They're hardly more than kittens. I don't know whether you'll like this one. She's a lot more skittish than the other."

Julie felt an instant empathy for the small frightened creature, its back stiff with fear. She too had experienced that same feeling of panic. She reached out and gently stroked the animal. "It's all right," she said, her voice soft and comforting. The cat turned around and stared at her with strange, sad eyes.

"She likes you," Laura said. "You must have a way with animals."

Julie was well aware that Laura's flattery was a deliberate part of her sales pitch, but somehow she didn't mind. How could you fault someone for trying to sell you something you wanted anyhow? And suddenly she *did* want this small animal for her own, to hold, cuddle, and reassure with tenderness. "What unusual eyes she has."

"You mean, because they're yellow?"

"No, not that . . . Actually, it's just one of her eyes. It looks strange—as though a child had drawn a few, thick, black eyelashes all around it."

"Oh, that—that's just her markings. I think it makes her look more interesting," Laura said, dismissing the point in an offhand way.

Julie hardly noticed. "I think I'll call her Daisy. That's

what her coloring and that eye of hers makes me think of."

Julie noticed with amusement that Laura didn't even bat an eye of her own at her triumph. The perfect salesperson. Or was *con artist* more like it? Laura merely said, "That's a super name. I couldn't think of anything that seemed just right. *Daisy* is perfect."

She gave the cat a loud buss on its nose as Julie mentally plotted how she could introduce the animal into her household. Her father was to pick her up after her driving lesson that afternoon. Together they would find a way to convince her mother that this special pet would give the house the one touch neglected by the decorator.

8

When Julie went out with Jeff on the following Monday, she'd already had a half-dozen driving lessons. Although she was still nervous behind the wheel, at least, she told herself, her shifting had improved. She was even beginning to feel that if she had the fortitude to stick with Jeff's instruction, one day she just might have a little of the mastery that seemed to come so easily to him. Today's lesson consisted of driving to the industrial park and practicing turns there as well as parking. She followed his directions conscientiously and was gratified to hear a few rare words of praise from him.

So far, all of their conversation had concerned only the business at hand, so that day, when she had finally parked to his satisfaction, and before she'd had the chance to put the car in motion again, she was surprised when he asked, "How is the cat doing?"

She'd taken Daisy home a week ago. Jeff had dropped her at his house that afternoon, then immediately taken off to run errands, so he wasn't in on the frantic moment of adoption. Poor Daisy, secured in a cardboard box, had wailed piteously all the way home.

Julie said, "She's doing as well as can be expected, I guess. Laura suggested that I start her out in my bedroom, so I did. Naturally she did the same thing with me that she did with her—she found a dark place to hide in my closet and stayed there all night."

"Is she eating?"

"She didn't that first night. It wasn't until the next morning that I lured her out of the closet with food. I guess she was so hungry by then she decided to brave it."

"If she's too much trouble, we'll be glad to take her back."

"Oh, she's doing much better. She's getting used to me, I think. She even slept on my feet last night. And now, when she gets scared, she's graduated to hiding under the bed, so, you see, she's making brilliant progress." She expected, at least, a trace of a smile, but Jeff only looked more concerned than ever.

He said, "Laura mentioned that you were worried your mother might not be all that keen about having a cat in the house."

Although Julie felt no conscious inclination to confide in him, she found herself saying, "Life's full of surprises. I've known my mother for seventeen years, and yet it wasn't until I brought Daisy home that I discovered that she'd had cats as a child. I guess you never really know anyone completely."

Her mother had commented, "Your grandfather used to say, 'How do you know it's a home if there isn't a big old cat lying around someplace.' No, I don't mind cats as long as they spend most of their time outdoors where they can't claw the furniture. If I'd known you wanted one, we could have looked for a Siamese."

"I want this one," Julie had said. Somehow winning the trust of the timorous animal had become an important challenge. Silly or not, she almost felt that if Daisy could love her that would prove—something.

She turned to Jeff now and said, "For better or worse, I guess poor little Daisy is a part of our household—unless, of course, she decides she doesn't want us."

"That's not likely," Jeff said. "Incidentally, what made you call her Daisy?"

"Mostly her yellow eyes—especially the one with the strange markings. My dad says it looks peculiar. He thinks I should have the vet check it when I take her for shots next week."

Jeff said quickly, "She doesn't need shots now. The people who gave her to us already took care of that. Laura should have told you."

"Where did they take her?"

With a note of suspicion in his voice, he said, "Why?"

Why, indeed, Julie thought, bristling at his manner. "Because anyone I take her to just might want to see her records."

"Oh. Well, I believe they took her to a man out near Mystic Valley."

"So far?"

"It wasn't far for them," he said shortly. "They live out that way."

Mystic Valley, the nearest town, must be at least thirty miles away, Julie thought. "I don't think my dad would want to drive that far when there are vets closer."

"I told you, you don't have to drive any place. The cat's already had shots. She won't need more for months and months."

Julie couldn't decide what it was she heard in his voice—

annoyance? anxiety? She recalled that Laura had acted a little strange too when they were talking about the cats. Was there something both Laura and Jeff weren't telling her? She decided to put her suspicions to the test. "Even if she has had shots, I'd still like her looked at. She keeps washing the side of her face with that funny eye. I think it irritates her."

"Look, if you think there's something wrong with the cat, I told you, we'd be glad to take it back. In fact, now that you bring it up, I think you're right." He avoided her eyes as he spoke, much the way Laura had on Friday. "Laura mentioned that the cat was working at one of its eyes a lot. She should never have let you take it. It's unfair to pass off an unhealthy animal on someone."

Julie was mystified. What was going on?

Jeff said, "I'll tell you what I'll do. I'll take the cat back today and find you a healthy kitten—maybe a Siamese if I can. How does that sound to you?"

The mention of a Siamese, almost as if he'd been privy to her mother's conversation, made her feel perverse. "That doesn't sound good at all. I don't *want* a Siamese. I'll keep the cat I have, thanks, and do just what I planned. I'll have a vet check her out."

He gave a long sigh and sank back in his seat, looking as if he might be debating some sensitive issue with himself. Finally he turned to her and said, "To be perfectly honest with you, Laura had no business giving you that animal. She simply didn't understand that the man who gave us the cats expected us to keep both of them. He did mention that they have a certain eye condition. He was only entrusting them to our care because he knew we'd take care of them if anything went wrong."

77

Puzzled, Julie said, "You mean there's something wrong with their sight?"

"No, not their sight. That's okay. They just have a little eyelid problem."

Julie stared at him curiously. What was he keeping from her? "I don't mind doing what I can for Daisy if she has a problem. As I said, I'll take her to see a vet and—"

"No!" Immediately after his outburst, he looked embarrassed. "I'm sorry. I didn't mean to come on so heavy, but you're not leaving me any choice. This concerns something that I don't want to get you involved in—I mean, something illegal. If you let me take the cat, you won't be a party to it."

Curiouser and curiouser, Julie thought. "I suspect I'm already involved." Joking, she asked, "Am I harboring stolen property?"

He shot her a startled look. "I didn't say that."

"You didn't have to. The way you're acting speaks for itself. What I don't understand is why anyone would steal cats, especially cats with something wrong with them, when you can't even give healthy ones away. I think you owe me an explanation."

He gave a long sigh. "I guess I do." He leaned toward her, a serious expression on his face. "Will you promise not to repeat what I say—not even to your family? I mean, this is something that could actually send some good people to jail."

Although she suspected Jeff was exaggerating, she decided to humor him. "All right. I promise."

"You're partly right, you know. Some people would call the cats stolen. We in the Animal Rights Society call them liberated."

Julie shook her head. "I don't understand. Who took them and from whom?"

"Not our society. We're not that kind of activists. The Animal Liberation Army took them. They've raided several well-known research labs and rescued as many animals as they could from cruel and senseless experiments. Our members have been helping them find homes for the animals."

So that was it. People *could* go to jail—including herself. "You mean Daisy was part of some research experiment?"

"Yes, and so was our cat. Both of them had one eye sewn shut."

Julie stared at him, unbelieving. "Why would anyone do something like that?"

"I don't know. Probably because the lab was doing some experiments on sight deprivation. They also had an infant macaque monkey which, their records say, they took from its mother at birth. They treated it differently from the cats— they sutured both its eyelids closed, then bandaged a heavy sonar device to its head."

Julie shuddered. "I find that hard to believe."

"Someday I'll introduce you to him. Fortunately, we were able to find him a surrogate mother, so he's doing okay now. His eyelids are permanently damaged though."

"You mean those aren't natural markings on Daisy's eye, but scars where her lids were stitched together?"

"That's right. Our vet said that medically the experimenters did a really sloppy job. They used a thick, coarse thread that wasn't even appropriate, so naturally it rubbed against the cornea and made the animals' eyes swollen and inflamed. Hardly anything you could call humane."

Julie felt sick. The thought of sewing anyone's eyelids together, animal or human, to force the creature to live in

79

a world of darkness was beyond her comprehension. Surely there had to be some vital reason. "Why was the experiment necessary?"

"It wasn't, as far as I'm concerned. After the raid, when things were made public, the experimenters said they were trying to find out if sonar devices could help children who were blind from birth. When reporters asked them why they didn't test the things on blind children instead of animals, they said they couldn't find any who lived close enough to their lab."

"Surely this couldn't have been an accredited laboratory!"

"Oh, yes, it was. I can't tell you its name, but it was in the Los Angeles area. And that wasn't the only stupid experiment going on there. They were doing all sorts of repetitious behavioral studies with animals when they could have obtained the same information from clinical studies that have already been done on human beings."

"But that's only one lab," Julie protested.

"I wish you were right. Unfortunately, all of the labs that our society knows about—and our information comes from people who work in them—do too many experiments that benefit no one. Not only that, but you would believe the reports we have on how unsanitary most of the labs are and how the animals are neglected."

"But if the experiments aren't necessary, why do they do them?"

"Well, in the case of university labs, it's a part of the publish or perish syndrome. These people write and publish papers on animal experimentation to get ahead academically. Other labs have other reasons they seem to find equally valid."

"I still find it hard to believe that anyone could bring

himself to sew up an animal's eyes for such a flimsy reason. How can people do something like that?"

"I suspect they desensitize themselves. They have to convince themselves that animals aren't feeling creatures. Actually, the monkey and the cats were lucky. The raiders found possums, not even old enough to leave their mothers' pouches, with brutal eye mutilations."

Again Julie shuddered.

Jeff said, "Now you know. You see why I didn't want you to take the cat to just any vet. There's always the chance of someone's connecting the cat's problem with the raid."

Julie nodded.

"If you don't want to get involved, you can do what I suggested—give the cat back to me."

"I have the feeling that I'm already involved—more so after hearing the story. Poor Daisy. I sort of feel I'd like to try to make things up to her."

"You don't mind sticking your neck out?"

Julie thought about it, then said jokingly, "No. From now on I'll just think of myself as living dangerously." When Jeff grinned at her, she had the feeling that she had reached him for the first time.

9

On Wednesday afternoon, driving home to give Julie another driving lesson, Jeff had a number of concerns on his mind, one of which was the subject of summer vacation. Until now he'd escaped committing himself. Much to his relief, his mother, caught up in some pressing problems on her job, had put aside all mention of the topic.

He assumed she'd forgotten the matter when, at dinner last night, she'd said to Laura, "A few days ago I told Jeff that the three of us should talk about going someplace special this summer, the way we used to in the old days."

Jeff noted the deep frown lines that immediately formed on Laura's forehead. "You mean, go camping?" she asked.

Jeff couldn't remember a summer while his father was alive that the whole family hadn't spent a portion of out in the wilds. As far as his father was concerned, the more remote the spot, the better. He loved nothing more than roughing it, spending hours combing the area for edible weeds that only he was willing to eat. Jeff felt a catch in his throat just thinking about it.

His mother said, "No, I didn't mean camping. That would be too sad a reminder. I thought we could try to find a summer rental in one of the beach towns for a couple of weeks."

"A couple of weeks!" Laura exclaimed. "I thought you meant a weekend."

Noreen Ryder's spine stiffened. "What's wrong with a couple of weeks I'd like to know? I have vacation time coming and you have the whole summer to fill."

"That's just it," Laura said. "I hope to fill it with some kind of job. If I'm going to college in the fall, I'm going to need all the extra money I can put my hands on. Besides, I'd like to spend as much time with Brian as I can. After all, we'll be going to different schools next year."

Jeff felt a foreboding as he watched the hurt look spread over his mother's face. "Well, forget it. It was just a suggestion. I simply thought it would be nice for the three of us to have a little time together away from the daily grind."

"I know, Mom. And it *would* be nice." Laura glanced pointedly at Jeff, obviously waiting for him to come to the rescue. When he deliberately offered nothing, she said, "It's just that if I get a job, my time won't be my own."

"*If* you get a job. You know, temporary jobs aren't always easy to find. Let's let it go for now. We'll wait and see how things work out," Noreen said. She gave Jeff a conspiratorial wink. "When you see Jeff and me packing our bathing suits and setting out with nothing more pressing on our minds than the gorgeous tans we plan to bring back, you'll just be so jealous, you won't be able to stand it."

Jeff's spirits sank. He'd thought that with Laura begging off, his mother would forget her plans, but no. He was still on the hook. He opened his mouth to bring up San Francisco and the law office he'd wanted to work in again this summer, then decided this was not the right moment. His refusal, coming right after Laura's, would make his mother feel totally abandoned. She'd had a hard enough time coping with life on her own.

Then he asked himself why he was making excuses for her. Laura was right. She should have friends her own age. With his need to make money to continue his schooling and the countless demands on his time, there were just about as many pressures as he could handle. He just couldn't take on the burden of feeling responsible for someone else's happiness, especially a parent's. He suspected he should face the issue head-on, yet he couldn't bring himself to do so. The summer was still a long way off, he reasoned. By that time anything could happen. The problem could simply disappear of itself.

Another matter that was bothering him was a commitment he'd made to Calvin Wallace, the managing director of the ARS. In the days when his father had been alive, Cal had been a frequent visitor to their home. He was divorced and childless and, in spite of running a busy automobile agency, had more time to devote to the ARS than Jeff's father. Because there was always some business for the two men to thrash out, Cal was often a dinner guest and, just as often, included in family outings. Jeff had never given the matter much thought then. Now he supposed that his father had felt sorry for the man.

Right after his father's death, Cal had tried to make himself available to the family for any help they needed. Strangely enough, his mother had firmly eased the man right out of their intimate lives. Jeff had never understood why. All she'd said was "While we have each other, we don't need the help of outsiders." From that time on, Cal had become more of an acquaintance than a friend. When he'd shown up out of the blue last night and said that he wanted to talk to Jeff, Jeff had assumed the matter must have something to do with the society, and he was right.

"There's something we'd like you to do for us," Cal had said.

"Oh?" For some reason, Jeff felt uneasy.

"There's a job coming up for a student in the university lab. We'd like you to apply for it, Jeff."

Jeff hesitated. "What kind of job?"

"Nothing you can't do—feeding, watering the lab animals—that sort of thing. Naturally, it doesn't pay much."

"How did you know about it?"

Cal, a muscular man with a shock of prematurely white hair, grinned. "Spies."

Jeff felt he should have known better than to ask. The society never divulged its sources. Cal said, "If your father were alive and still teaching there, I know he'd do anything he could for us. As it is, we thought *you* might like to help."

Cal was right. His father had been totally dedicated to the society and their cause. "What's the deal?"

Cal's face grew serious. "For a long time now we've been hearing rumors that the psychology lab leaves a lot to be desired. We think it's time to check it out and find out for ourselves."

"And then what?"

"We'll decide that when we know what's going on. Will you do it?"

Jeff thought the matter over for a moment. Although he

had asked *and then what,* he was well aware of the answer. His lab findings, if unacceptable to those in the society, could well provoke another Animal Liberation Army raid.

Would his father have made the same request of him? he asked himself. He wasn't sure. He recalled the time one of his science teachers had talked about animal experimentation. "It's done purely for the benefit of all mankind," he'd said. "This is one instance where the end certainly justifies the means."

When Jeff had asked his father what he thought of the teacher's statement, his father had answered, "I'd have to ask myself *what ends* and *what means* he was talking about. And the answer is something you're going to have to think through for yourself if it's to have any meaning for you." That was so like his dad. He had never tried to shove his own ethics down his children's throats.

Does the end justify the means? He'd thought about the question many times but had never come to any definite conclusion. As his father had said, the answer depended too much on what ends and what means.

He could see no reason for saying no to Cal. After all, the lab received government funding. If the place was inadequate, someone should certainly know. He said, "I'll do it if I can get the job. A lot of other guys want part-time work too, so it may not be all that easy."

"Just try," Cal said. "That's all we can ask."

And early that morning, that was what Jeff had done. Apparently Cal's information was right. There *was* an opening coming up in the near future. Although the professor he'd spoken to had made no definite commitment, Jeff had the feeling that he was considered suitable for the job and would probably get it. Now he almost hoped they'd decide

86

upon someone else. He hated the idea of spying, even if it was for a worthy cause.

There was something else on his mind that day, a pleasanter concern. Julie. He couldn't stop thinking about her. She wasn't at all like his preconceived notion of a model. At first he'd been surprised at how shy she'd seemed. You'd never dream that someone who had spent most of her life posing for photographers, and undoubtedly receiving all the adulation that had to go with that kind of work, could be so timid. On the other hand, she had certainly stood her ground when she wanted to keep that cat, so she wasn't exactly a wimp.

Until then, he had felt only hostility toward her. She was just someone he had to put up with for the time being to earn extra money, someone so totally superficial she couldn't possibly grapple with a serious or intellectual thought. Although bragging to the guys at school about teaching *the* Julie Peters to drive had occurred to him, he had rejected the idea. *They* might have been impressed, but he would have felt that he was behaving like a high school kid rather than a college man. If anything, he wanted to feel he was a person who could appreciate substance rather than something only as skin-deep as looks.

So much for high thoughts, he decided. Prejudice was more like it. On Monday, all his warped notions had disappeared. Now Julie and he were partners in crime, to put it melodramatically. He still couldn't get over the fact that she was willing to involve herself in something risky, something she could have backed out of so easily.

With new interest in her, he'd spent a good portion of last night in the garage, going through women's magazines that over the past six months his sister and mother had saved for some charity. To his surprise he couldn't find one picture of Julie until he came across an issue of *Seventeen* that was over a year old. Somehow it had found its way into the stack. There she was on the cover, wearing lots of eye makeup, looking a bit too brazen and seductive for his taste. He took the copy to stash away in the desk drawer that held his really private papers, then kept pulling it out again and again that night.

Now as he directed the Mustang into the driveway of his house, he spotted her sitting on the front steps alone, obviously waiting for him. When she saw him, she jumped up and made for the car. He got out, with the engine still running, and let her take the driver's seat, then went around and slid in the other side.

"Do you mean to tell me Laura left you outside all by yourself?" he asked, annoyed with his sister's thoughtlessness.

"I just came out this minute," Julie said. "We were inside playing with Jenny, but I know you don't like to waste any more time than you have to, so I thought I'd wait out here."

Was that the impression he'd given her? "I didn't mean to make you feel like I think I'm doing you a favor. It's *your* time I've been thinking of. I mean, I want you to feel that you're getting your money's worth."

"Oh, I do. In fact, I think you're underpaid. Anyone who'd take on someone as slow as I am when it comes to machinery has got to be a glutton for punishment."

"Hey, you're not that slow. In fact, you're doing so well I thought maybe you'd like to try a little long-distance driving today. We can take the road to Mystic Valley. That's never very busy."

"Doesn't that road wind up in the desert?"

"Uh-huh. But we don't have to go that far." Jeff began to toy with the idea of showing her Mercedes Damsen's animal refuge, which was out that way. His better judgment told him he would be taking an unnecessary chance. What are you trying to do, sell her a bill of goods? he asked himself. God forbid. He couldn't stand it when people tried to do something like that to him, so why should he pull the same thing on her?

Besides, what made him think he could trust her? The cat was one thing. This was something else, something that involved other people. No, they would simply head out toward the desert but turn back well before they got to Mercedes's place. "You can use some practice in sustained driving," he told her.

She had never been on that road, so he directed her to the highway. When they were well along the way, she said, "It's strange how quickly all the greenery disappears. It's so barren out here."

"Santa Delores is really a man-made town. It's only because they can bring water in from the north that we have a town here at all. Otherwise it would only be one big hunk of desert."

They drove for a while in silence, Julie's eyes fastened to the white lines in the pavement, Jeff sneaking a look at her profile. She had beautiful skin, he noticed, and thick black lashes that were obviously her own. Her long, blond hair was tied back artlessly with a ribbon. If she wore any makeup at all, he certainly couldn't detect it. He liked this girl so much better than the one with all the eye goo on the cover of *Seventeen*.

"How am I doing?" she asked.

"Great." On the whole, he thought, this highway with its

light traffic seemed an ideal road for the beginning driver. Julie appeared surer of herself today, so Jeff relaxed back into his seat, feeling more expansive than usual. "You know," he said, "something I've been meaning to do for a long time now is apologize to you."

"Apologize? For what?"

"For giving your name to the press during the demonstration that Laura managed to pull you into. We both acted like jerks—especially me."

Julie was silent for so long that Jeff wondered if she'd heard him. Finally, she said, "To tell you the truth, I was pretty mad at the time. You don't have to apologize though. I think I understand now why you did it."

"But I *do* have to apologize—I want to apologize." Then, trying to make light of something that had been hard to bring himself to do, he added, "In fact, you're not supposed to be so blasted forgiving. You're supposed to tell me I was way out of line and that you want me to live with the guilt for the rest of my life."

"All right. You were way out of line and I hope you feel guilty for the rest of your life."

She sounded so completely serious he stared at her for a moment, almost prepared to feel properly chastened. Then she took her eyes from the road just long enough to glance his way and break into a smile. He was surprised at the feeling of relief that flooded through him. He matched her smile and in another moment they both began to laugh.

Finally she sobered and said, "I mustn't laugh. I can't laugh and drive too. I can only concentrate on one thing at a time."

"Something else I've been meaning to tell you—your driving is really a lot better. Shouldn't be too long before you're ready to try for your license."

"Oooh, that really makes me feel nervous—just thinking about it," she said, but he thought she looked pleased.

Then she fell silent. At length she said, "You know, it's all Laura's doing."

"What's all Laura's doing?"

"I mean, she's been giving me all kinds of pamphlets about the awful way people treat animals. It makes me understand better why you both feel the way you do."

"That's Laura for you. She loves to preach. What's she been showing you?"

"Oh, there was one pamphlet about something called the LD50 test that's supposed to determine the lethal dose of a substance. They force-feed animals household chemicals until fifty percent of them die—in agony, it said."

"Did she show you the one about the Draize test?"

"No."

"That's the one where they take the toxic products we use around the house and pour them into the eyes of rabbits. Then some conscientious researcher puts down careful notes on how long it takes for the eye to deteriorate."

Julie shuddered. "I don't understand how people can bring themselves to make innocent creatures—animal or human— suffer like that."

"I know. In the old days people used to sacrifice animals— and even human beings sometimes—to the gods. Now we know *that* was senseless. Maybe someday we'll realize that this is senseless too."

"I certainly hope so," Julie said.

Once more they drove in silence. Jeff couldn't help wondering what she thought of him. Probably thought he was a nerd—a real small-town rube. On the other hand, she was still in high school while he was already a college man. That should even things up a bit. He stared out the window with a sudden sense of heightened awareness. The day was a perfect one with a sky so clear that the distant mountains, seldom visible, were cleanly etched against the horizon. Even the highway stretched ahead invitingly, suggesting adventure and discovery.

Jeff said, "I said that sometime I'd introduce you to the monkey the ALA rescued. How would you like to meet him today?"

Julie glanced quickly his way. "You mean the one that had both his eyes sewn shut?"

"The very same." He couldn't quite read her expression. Surprised? Flattered maybe?

She said softly, "I'd love to see him."

She smiled and Jeff, in spite of his earlier resolution, found himself giving her directions to Mercedes Damsen's place.

10

Julie drove Jeff's Mustang carefully along the bumpy gravel driveway that led back to a weathered ranch house. The place was at the edge of the desert, some distance from the last vestiges of civilization. Before the car neared the building, the frantic barking of what sounded like a huge kennel of dogs announced their arrival.

"Mercedes doesn't need to worry about being surprised by burglars," Jeff said. "Not with thirty or forty dogs always around."

"So many?" Julie exclaimed.

"I should tell you that the place is full of throwaway animals—a lot of them wild. People get exotic pets when they're small, then find they can't handle them as they grow. The only reason the city gave Mercedes a license to run this menagerie is because she's so far from town."

"If what she's doing is legal, why would she take in an animal like a monkey that she had to know was stolen?"

"Liberated—remember?"

"All right—liberated."

93

Jeff said, "Groups like ours take advantage of her, because we know she'd never turn away an animal in need. Her place provides a good cover for us. It's kind of a halfway house for mistreated animals until she can find a permanent home for some of them."

As Julie pulled to a stop in front of the long covered porch and turned off the ignition, Jeff turned to her and looked deeply into her eyes. "You realize that I'm telling you this in confidence."

"Of course. I won't repeat a word—don't worry." All the flattery she'd received in her life was as nothing compared to being treated like a person who could be trusted.

Before either of them could say another word, a thin, wiry woman of about fifty in well-worn jeans, a golden retriever at her heels, emerged from the house. "That's Mercedes," Jeff said. As he got out of the car, the dog made a beeline for him to greet him by jumping all over him and plastering his face with sloppy kisses.

"Down, Essex, down, you incorrigible hound," Mercedes demanded. She left the porch to meet Jeff and offer her hand. Julie saw him say something to her in a voice too low to hear. Mercedes nodded, and Jeff turned back toward the car, beckoned, and called, "Come on, Julie."

Julie joined him and received a thorough sniffing from Essex, for which he was immediately reprimanded by Mercedes. "Come here, you beast," she said in a voice that tolerated more than it scolded.

Jeff introduced Julie to the woman and said, "She's one of us, Mercedes." To Julie's relief, Mercedes was apparently not up on teenage models. She smiled, shook Julie's hand firmly, and said, "Any friend of the ARS is welcome here. Jeff tells me that you took in one of our cats."

So they had initially wound up here. "Yes, and she's doing really well now."

"Good. I love happy endings."

Jeff said, "I promised Julie she'd get to meet Butch."

Mercedes shook her head, a look of mock concern on her face. "That little dickens is getting too sassy for his britches." She opened the front door and invited them in. As she ushered them through the house, Julie decided that Mercedes was an especially handsome woman. Her aquamarine-blue eyes sparkled in a deeply tanned face. Although her sun-bleached blond hair was now vying with gray and losing the battle, she must have been very beautiful when she was younger, Julie thought.

As if he'd been reading her mind, Jeff said, "Mercedes used to be an actress."

Mercedes laughed, flashing a row of even white teeth. "I wasn't bad either."

"Were you in films?" Julie asked.

"A few. Mostly my work was in the theater—but that was quite a while back."

"Did you give it up?" Julie asked, curious now.

"Yes, I gave it up. You might say I found a higher calling that takes all my time."

Somehow Julie couldn't restrain herself. "But don't you miss it?"

Mercedes smiled. "Not a bit. I think I only went into the business because it was expected of me. Everyone said I looked like an actress. Well, maybe I did back then, but I wasn't a natural. I never loved acting the way so many people do. To tell you the truth, playing the same role night after night after night bored the very devil out of me."

Julie was astonished. Here was a woman who seemed to

95

feel exactly the way she did. And with no apologies. How incredible! And yet, how many people would have called Mercedes Damsen a fool?

Julie had no time to ponder the many interesting facets of the subject, because Mercedes said, "Follow me, you two," and led them through a hallway and out the back door, making sure Essex was safely secured inside the house.

She gave them a quick tour of what she called the zoo. And, indeed, it was a zoo with roomy cages that, among other animals, held a tiger and a pair of leopards that looked almost full-grown. The dogs, who were still barking nervously at the sound and smell of strangers, were kept in kennels with long runs.

"We even have a couple of wolf dogs here," Mercedes told Julie. "We keep them by themselves where they can't breed. Lord knows where the people who brought them in got them, but they took them as pups and then found out when they grew that they weren't to be trusted as pets." Mercedes gave a disgusted shake of her head. "People can be idiots."

Now and then Julie spotted domestic cats roaming about freely or skittering out of the way of the visitors. Mercedes said, "They have the run of the place. Sometimes they disappear for hours, but, believe me, they all turn up for meal-time."

There were several other people working there who Mercedes told Julie were volunteers. "I don't know what I'd do without them," she said.

She led Julie and Jeff to the rear of the property where huge cages held what looked to Julie like families of primates.

"Look, there's Butch," Jeff said, pointing out a tiny monkey who clung to another many times his size and much darker in color.

Mercedes said, "I'd take him out to visit with you, but he's just beginning to feel secure, even to the point of playing tricks on his surrogate mother now. She's not his same species, but he doesn't know that, and she doesn't care."

Julie thought he was just about the cutest thing she had ever seen, even though the scars on his eyelids were still visible from where she stood.

"Blossom, bless her big heart, just loves to play mother. She even took a kitten under her wing once," Mercedes said.

The little monkey glanced at the visitors. His formerly sightless eyes, big and innocent, fastened on Julie, taking her in, she thought, like a creature entranced with the newness of a world so full of interesting objects. How vulnerable he looked. But now he had a mother, someone he could trust, someone who would never use him for anyone's benefit but his own. Julie said to Mercedes, "It's really wonderful what you're doing."

"Not really. I'm just a sucker for animals. Besides, there are plenty of people who help humans. Somebody has to stand by the animal kingdom if we're ever to call ourselves civilized."

Jeff and Julie spent a good half hour visiting. When they were ready to leave, Mercedes said, "You're welcome to drop in anytime, Julie. Just give me a call first."

"Thanks, I'd love to. Maybe when I get my license." Julie felt pleased that anyone as intriguing as Mercedes, a woman who seemed to have her life so comfortably together, would even bother to invite her back.

When she and Jeff headed toward town, Jeff said, "To-day's lesson is on me. After all, it was my idea that we waste so much of your driving time."

"That doesn't matter." She wanted to say, *Thank you for trusting me and for introducing me to Mercedes. You can't imagine how good it feels to know there is someone dedicated to rescuing the helpless from people who believe some creatures exist only for the benefit of others.* Instead, she said, "Besides, I drove all the way out here, and I'm driving back, so I'm getting my driving time in anyhow."

"Now, don't argue about it—okay?"

Something about his tone told Julie he would only be offended if she insisted on paying him, so she shrugged and said, "Okay."

"Besides," Jeff said, "I have another idea for wasting more time."

Julie glanced at him curiously. "Oh?"

He leaned forward in his seat and pointed toward a side road coming up that took off from the highway and disappeared into a gully that looked greener than the rest of the countryside. "Take a right there. I want to show you something."

Wondering what he had in mind, Julie obeyed and found herself on a long, narrow lane, heading toward a grove of trees. She kept driving until they reached a dead end where Jeff told her to park. They got out of the car, and he led her through the brush and down to a small, hidden creek, shaded by tall cottonwood and eucalyptus trees.

"Most people don't know this is here," Jeff said. "They use a park closer to town for picnics. My family always preferred this spot, because we had it to ourselves."

The place looked like an oasis in the desert, Julie thought. "I wonder why other people don't come here."

"No incentive. The park has fire pits and a man-made pond that has water all year round." He nodded toward the creek. "In a couple of months this will be nothing but a dry bed."

"It's nice now though—peaceful."

"Yeah, I like it." He sat down on one end of a fallen tree trunk that looked as if it had been there since the world began and patted the area beside him. "Try it. It's so worn away it doesn't feel bad." As Julie joined him, he added, "It's a good spot to watch the clouds in the water and contemplate nature. That is, when there *are* clouds and when there *is* water."

They sat in silence for a moment, the only sound the soft rustle of wind in the trees, the air full of the aromatic scent of eucalyptus leaves. Finally Julie mused, "I wonder how Mercedes can afford to run a place that certainly doesn't exist for making money."

"Oh, her parents left her fairly well off, I understand. Besides that, she gets donations from individuals and from some of the animal groups."

"It's hard to understand though how she could leave an acting career. I mean, most people think that someone in a job like that is so lucky. I don't know how she ever brought herself to turn her back on it."

Jeff, his eyes on the ground, scraped the earth around with his foot. "I don't know. I can understand how someone can get into a certain kind of work though and then find out that they'd rather do something else. After all, sometimes you can't know what you want until you try it."

"I suppose so."

"How about you? According to Laura, most girls would sell their souls for a modeling career, and yet, she tells me, you want to go to college instead."

Although, in her heart, she had felt a kinship to Mercedes Damsen, Julie hadn't expected Jeff to use her comments to probe a very sensitive spot inside her. She said, somewhat defensively, "Going to college doesn't mean I can't take modeling jobs now and then."

"Is that what you plan on doing?"

Julie hesitated. The subject was one she had been trying to avoid thinking about for a long, long time. "I don't know."

"Why don't you know?"

Julie felt her skin prickle. "You're very direct, aren't you?" she said, hedging.

"I suppose I am." Without backing down, he repeated, "Why don't you know?"

"I don't know because"—she shrugged—"because I don't know."

"Do you want to go back to modeling?"

She tossed her head indifferently. "I guess so."

"You're not sure?"

Why did he have to persist so? "I seem to be successful at it. Everyone says so."

"Who's everyone?"

He was really pinning her down, and she didn't like the feeling. "Well, my agent—and the people who hire me—and the public, I guess. And, of course, my parents." Perhaps she was wrong in including her father, but then, he usually went along with whatever her mother wanted. Certainly he had never objected.

100

"Strange," Jeff said. "Laura seemed to have the impression that you were through with that part of your life."

"I never told her that," Julie said shortly. "Besides, it's what I do best. My mother says so. And my agent says so."

Jeff looked at her quizzically. "You sound a little like Mercedes—you look the part, so everyone expects it of you, and that's what you do. What about you? Is it what *you* want to do?"

Julie shrugged. "Why not?"

Jeff stared at her for a long moment. "Why do I get the feeling that you're not exactly jumping for joy at the thought?"

Julie shifted uncomfortably. "Why would I jump for joy? I mean, modeling is just something I've done forever, it seems. You don't get excited about something you've done forever. I mean, people just tell you what to do, and you do it. It's nothing to go into raptures about. You might as well be a piece of meat for all anyone—" She broke off, suddenly aware that, in the heat of the moment, she had revealed more of herself than she had intended.

Jeff said softly, "You don't like the work at all, do you?"

Again she grew defensive. "How could I not like something that—as you said yourself—so many girls would give their souls to do?" She couldn't keep a touch of irony from her tone. "My mother says I'm one of the lucky ones. My agent says I'm one of the lucky ones."

"But you don't think so."

In a small voice, she found herself saying, "I'd rather do almost anything else." She gave a deep sigh. "But it means so much to my mother."

He gave her an almost startled look. After a moment he said, "What about your father?"

101

Julie smiled. "My father is the sweetest, kindest, gentlest person in the whole world—a real pussycat—but he's so involved in his work that, whether he realizes it or not, he's happy to have my mother run not only the house but our lives."

"I guess he wouldn't be much help then. What about you? Do you have any thought about what you do want to do?"

"I don't know exactly. I've been thinking about it, and the truth is I think I'm something of a scholar." When she saw Jeff's eyebrows lift, she added quickly, "Oh, I don't mean I'm brilliant or anything like that, although I always did pretty well with my tutors. They thought my grade average would give me a good choice of schools. I mean, I just want to know about things like dead languages and ancient civilizations. Mostly I want the time to dip into all the subjects that interest me until I find out where I do belong." When the words were out, she couldn't believe that they had come from her.

They were both silent for a time. Finally, Jeff said, "I'm a fine one to talk about doing what *you* want to do. I seem to have much the same problem as you." When Julie looked at him questioningly, he added, "Until last summer I thought I knew exactly where I was going and exactly what I wanted to be."

"Laura says you're going to be a wildlife biologist."

He nodded. "That's what I thought. My dad was a botanist. He used to say that if he'd had it to do over, he'd have been a wildlife biologist instead. Before I was even old enough to know what that was, I told everyone that that was what I was going to be when I grew up. Then I kind of forgot about it until my dad died. After that, I decided that was the one thing I could do for him."

"You said something about last summer. What happened then?"

"Oh, I needed money for school, so my uncle put me to work in his law office in San Francisco. It was the weirdest thing. I'd never had the slightest interest in law, yet I found myself getting fascinated with it."

"What kind of lawyer is he? I mean, does he handle criminal cases, or what?"

"Civil cases. I think I drove him nuts asking questions. He was nice, though. He explained what he was trying to accomplish with each case that came along. It sounded really exciting to me—going into court, pleading a case, trying to win judgments for people you believe are getting raw deals, fighting it out. I think that's the kind of war—the only kind—I'd like to do battle in."

"Are you going to change your major then?"

Jeff, who had just sounded so animated and upbeat, said flatly, "I don't know." He gave Julie the flicker of a smile. "I told you, my problem is pretty much the same as yours."

"Your mother?"

"Yes, my mother. I won't go as far as to say it would break her heart, but it would sure disappoint her. She doesn't think too much of my uncle, even though he's her own brother. I don't think she knows the first thing about his work, but she usually calls him a shyster. She says she's just kidding, but you can tell she really feels that way."

Only yesterday, Julie would have said that she and Jeff had almost nothing in common. Now, sharing a problem, she felt very close to him. "What are you going to do about it?"

He shrugged. "I wish I knew. I'll have to make a decision pretty soon though."

At least Jeff sounded as if the decision was his to make. Julie always assumed that decisions were something that were made for her and her only part in the effort was to live up to them. She said, "I hope you'll give law a fair chance. You said yourself that you can't always know what you want to do until you try it."

He smiled at her, and for the first time, Julie really took him in. The Ryders were all good-looking people with their jet-black hair, fair skin, and deep blue, almost violet, eyes. Jeff was the tall one of the three and a little too thin, which sharpened his cheekbones and gave his face an angular, somewhat gaunt look that saved him from being handsome.

Julie said, "I hope you'll let me know what you decide." She thought, Maybe that will give me the courage I need to do what I want to do.

"It's a deal," he said, then added, "Enough of all that serious talk." He got up and helped her to her feet. "I just had a brilliant idea."

"What's that?"

"Well, you're almost ready to take your driver's exam. We'll set it up for a week from this Friday. That should give you enough practice time. If you pass it, on Saturday we'll pack a picnic lunch and come out here to celebrate."

"What if I flunk it?"

"We'll celebrate anyhow."

"Celebrate what?"

"Anything. The vernal equinox. Or the fact that the powers-that-be are benevolent enough to let flunkers take the driving test again. How about it?"

We? Surely he wasn't asking her on a picnic all by herself. After all, Laura was the one who had arranged the driving lessons. He would obviously include her in any celebration.

Wouldn't he? Julie said, "We'll have to check with Laura to see when she can make it."

"Oh, Laura—oh, sure. She can bring Brian along. They're both real big for celebrations."

He had hesitated just long enough to make her wonder if he *had* intended to ask Laura. "All right," she said. "Pass or fail—it's a deal."

"Good." As they walked to the car, he said, "Julie . . . Short for Julia?"

"Uh-uh—Juliette."

His brows climbed up his forehead in mock exaggeration. "Just shows you how far off the track you can be when you take things for granted."

Julie said, "Jeff—short for Jeffrey?"

He grinned. "Uh-uh—Jefferson."

She shook her head. "Just shows you—" she started to say, and they both broke up.

Later that evening, when Julie checked her calendar, she realized that her eighteenth birthday fell on the Sunday after their planned picnic. Wonderful, she thought. If she passed the test, there would be twice as much reason to celebrate.

11

At dinner with his mother and Laura that night Jeff was preoccupied, thinking about Julie. Until now, he had rarely seen her smile, but that afternoon laughter had lit up her face with a wonderful glow. Better yet, the crinkles at the corners of her usually serious gray eyes suggested a sense of humor he hadn't even suspected was there. Oh, man, talk about being way off the track! Talk about prejudging someone. Talk about surprises.

Like her name. *Juliette.* Nice. Romantic. Right out of Shakespeare. You seldom heard anyone called Juliette these days. Sort of took you back in time. He could picture her in medieval robes, all white and silver and pristine. She'd look gorgeous. Yet no matter how gorgeous she might look in person or in his imagination, he still could not equate the girl he was getting to know with the girl on the cover of the magazine in his drawer.

In every way, except for her looks, Julie was a far cry from what he supposed most models were like. She wasn't even like your average high school senior coed who couldn't see much beyond prom night. Not at all. Julie was sensitive—you could tell. And thoughtful—in her own judgment, a scholar. You'd certainly go a long way before you'd find another girl in a business like hers who was interested in dead languages! She was sympathetic, a good listener, and someone he'd definitely like to know better.

He didn't think much of his chances though. He'd practically come right out and asked her for a date only to have her immediately drag Laura into the picture. Which had to mean she wanted to keep things between him and her platonic. And when all was said and done, that was just as well. After all, he was always hurting for money, so he could never do anything extravagant for a date—the kind of thing she was undoubtedly used to. And look who she was! She'd probably never dated anyone who wasn't a celebrity. Still, he *was* a college man while she was only a high school senior. Would that weigh heavily enough on the plus side?

Well, even if it did, with years of schooling ahead, he was in no position to even consider involvement of that kind right now. And when you got right down to it, he wasn't thinking in those terms anyhow. What he really had in mind was something more like friendship with an occasional date. Maybe she'd appreciate that kind of relationship. After all, neither of them was tied up with anyone else right now, and even someone as special as Julie might need an escort once in a while.

His mother, on her after-dinner coffee now, broke into his thoughts. "How did the driving lesson go today?"

"Great," Jeff said. "In fact, Julie's doing so well she's almost ready to take her driving test. I think she can give it a try a week from Friday."

"Sounds like you've almost worked yourself out of a job,"

Laura said. "I thought you'd try to string things out as long as you could. After all, think of what most guys would give to be in your shoes."

Her mother turned a disapproving eye on her. "For heaven's sake, Laura, you know Jeff better than that. He has more important things on his mind than girls right now. Besides, the sooner he finishes up with her, the better. He has too many jobs going as it is."

Laura gave him a snide smile. "More important things on his mind than girls? I'll bet."

Usually Laura declared him ready for the priesthood because he lacked a serious girlfriend. Could Julie have said something to her after they'd returned from the driving lesson? Somehow he thought not.

His mother said lightly, "Don't pay any attention to Laura, Jeff. She thinks everyone's like her."

"Who, me?" Laura said innocently. "I don't have girls on my mind."

Instead of falling into Laura's joking mood, her mother said, "No, you have Brian on your mind. And too much so, if you ask me." Before she could continue, the phone sounded. "I'll get it," she said, and got up and made for the hall.

Laura made a face and mimicked her mother. "You have Brian on your mind. And too much so, if you ask me. Who asked her?"

"Now don't start," Jeff said. "Let's keep the peace. I just hope Brian isn't coming over tonight."

"Don't worry. We've cut back to three nights a week." She leaned forward in her chair with the air of one confiding an important secret. "I'd never say this to Mom, but, to tell you the truth, I like this arrangement better. I find I'm enjoying the time I have to myself, and by not seeing so much of Brian, I appreciate him just that much more."

"Mother knows best, I guess," Jeff said with a smile.

Laura dismissed the words with "I really didn't need Mom to suggest it. I was coming to the same conclusion myself. I just like to feel that I'm doing things of my own free will and not being forced."

Jeff, not wanting to take sides on an issue he found unimportant, said, "I understand," and changed the subject. "Julie and I decided—"

"Ah ha!" Laura exclaimed knowingly. "So now it's Julie and I."

"Aw, come on, Laura. Don't make something out of this that isn't there. I was about to say that if Julie passes her driving test—and I'm sure she will—we're going to celebrate. After all, getting a license is really an occasion."

"Humph. Nobody thought it an occasion when I got mine."

Laura had fallen into such a testy mood, Jeff was almost sorry he'd brought up the subject. To mollify her, he said, "That's twice as much reason for a celebration. We'll celebrate both your licenses. We'll have a picnic at the creek that Saturday. Naturally Brian's included."

Laura's mood immediately changed. "That's a great idea. Do you realize how long it's been since either one of us has been on a picnic?"

Not since before Dad died, Jeff thought. He said, "Too long."

Laura said, "We can't have a fire there, so we'll have to have sandwiches and fruit and salad. I might even make a cake."

Before he could respond, Noreen Ryder strode back into

109

the kitchen and took her place at the table again to finish her coffee. "That was Calvin Wallace," she said. "Apparently the ARS has lost one of its clerical volunteers and he wants me to take her place. Fortunately, she only worked one night a week."

"Does that mean you said yes?" Laura asked.

"I said I'd do it every Wednesday night until they can get someone else. After all, I'd have done the same thing for your father—and *did*—many times."

"Why Wednesday nights?" Jeff asked.

"Because that's the night *you* work, naturally."

He worked at the Bagel Machine Wednesday nights, but so what? "Why naturally? What's my working got to do with it?"

"Only that I like to be home when you're here."

"What about me?" Laura asked.

"You, too."

Jeff said, "You make me feel like I need a baby-sitter."

His mother looked hurt. "Is there some reason why I shouldn't enjoy being at home with my kids?"

How could you argue with that? Jeff thought. Neither he nor Laura said a word although he noticed that Laura was giving him a very meaningful look.

Noreen turned to Laura and said, "What did I miss while I was on the phone? I heard you say you were going to make a cake. What's the occasion?"

Laura told her about the picnic Jeff had planned for Julie and the reason for it. "We thought we'd all go to the creek, because we haven't been there in ages. And Brian's never been there."

Noreen said, "That's a wonderful idea." She turned to Jeff. "It's very thoughtful of you to do something that nice

110

for your pupil. Any excuse to have a party, I always say. And, come to think of it, it's about time we started doing things like that again."

We? Surely she didn't mean that the way it sounded. He said, "We didn't think you'd want to come, Mom. We thought it might bring back too many sad memories."

"Nonsense. It's about time I started getting over that sort of thing, isn't it?"

What could he say? If he came right out and told her she was unwanted, she would be devastated. Even Laura seemed to realize that they were stuck with the situation. Jeff could tell by the look she gave him.

And to think that all he had wanted was an excuse to spend some time alone with Julie!

12

At dinner in the Peterses' house that night, Julie's mind was busy going over the events of the afternoon, especially those moments when she and Jeff had exchanged confidences. Sharing her secret thoughts with another person had never come easy to her and she guessed the same was true of him. What had possessed them? Was there some magic about that particular spot that made people open up and confess their hidden fears? Whatever it was, the experience was very special.

She asked herself again if his idea for a picnic had been an excuse to try and date her. Probably not, she decided. Until now, their relationship had been, if not an icy one, definitely cool. There was not even the slightest indication that Jeff found her attractive as a female. If anything, he was probably making a gesture to let her know she was acceptable as a sort of friend. Which wasn't all that bad really. In fact, it was flattering—better than anything Morgan had prepared her to expect.

Over the years, she had often received mail, in care of her

agent, from adolescent boys, some expressing fantasies that bordered on the pornographic, others declaring undying love. Morgan had set her straight on all of them. "Don't get the idea that this has anything to do with reality," she'd said. "It's much easier for kids that age to deal with a picture than with the real thing. You're just about as substantial to them as Disney's Snow White."

Morgan had also warned her about what to expect as she grew older. "As a professional model, you'll have to guard against men who only want to show you off. These are the kind of guys who drive Ferraris and take you places where they're sure to be seen. They think it adds to their status."

Well, you certainly couldn't include Jeff in that category. Instead of choosing a public place like a restaurant to celebrate, he'd opted for a picnic at a spot that was just about as private as you could get. Perhaps he was ashamed to be seen with her just because she *was* something of a celebrity. If it worked one way, it probably worked the other. Then she chided herself. Would she ever get over analyzing and dissecting everyone's motives?

She ate her meal absently, hardly noticing what was on her plate until her father said to her mother, "This curried chicken is delicious. If this is one of Georgette's concoctions, I hope you plan to hang on to her."

"I think she'll work out," Anne Peters said, "if I can just get her to cut out all the fattening sauces she's been making." With her fork, she pointed to the chicken dish on her plate. "This probably has a thousand calories per teaspoon."

Poor Georgette Nacamoto, Julie thought, obviously so proud of her training in French cookery, but soon to be retrained in the Anne Peters school. "I thought the Japanese were big for vegetable dishes."

113

"Don't forget," her mother reminded her, "Georgette's half French. I understand she's an excellent oriental cook, but she seems to take more pride in what she learned in that French school she went to."

"Probably sees herself as another Julia Child," Harrison Peters said.

Julie picked out the chunks of chicken from the curried dish and pushed them to one side. "The Ryders are vegetarians. Did I tell you?"

"For health's sake, we could probably all do with less red meat," her father said.

Julie looked down at her plate. "The Ryders don't even eat chicken."

Her mother sniffed. "Good Lord, if you can't eat chicken and you can't eat meat, what's left? I just wish you wouldn't hang out with that Ryder girl so much. That whole family sounds like a bunch of weirdos."

"Why? Just because they're vegetarians?" Julie asked.

"Not only that but the girl—what's her name?"

"Laura."

"Yes, Laura. She was demonstrating downtown that day over a silly thing like a fur sale."

"Oh, kids love to feel they're doing something radical," Harrison Peters said.

Julie bristled. "She wasn't doing it because she wanted to do something radical. She was doing it because that's something she believes in. They all do. If that's extreme, then I can't see anything wrong with being extreme."

Her father, the peacemaker, said. "Calm down, Julie. I'm sure your mother wasn't criticizing them for the way they eat. Some of the world's greats were vegetarians—George Bernard Shaw, Leo Tolstoy, Leonardo da Vinci, to name a few. I have nothing against people who don't care to eat meat. I don't care to eat some of it myself—liver for example." He grinned at Julie's mother. "As you very well know. But meat versus vegetables is not a battle I want to waste my energy on. Don't forget, Julie, since the world began, one animal has always been food for another. You can't quarrel with nature's rules."

Julie wanted to say, *Laura says all the other primates are fundamentally vegetarians, which proves that that's a natural diet for humans too,* but she remained silent. There was no point in arguing. Instead, she changed the subject, hoping to prepare them for the forthcoming picnic. "Are you going to work every weekend, Dad?" she asked him. Ever since they'd been out here, he'd immersed himself in his project, even to the point of going in on Saturdays and Sundays. He was so absentminded she wondered if he even remembered her birthday.

"Suppose so."

"Your father's a workaholic," her mother said.

He'd always been like that, Julie thought, always involved in studies that tied him to the classroom, even when his breaks coincided with hers. And he would never discuss his research with anyone, not even her and her mother, until he'd published a paper on it or could declare it a triumph.

"Why? Something going on I should know about?" he asked Julie.

"Not really. Of course I *do* have a birthday coming up a week from Sunday. I bet you forgot."

"Whoops," he said and smiled sheepishly. "Well, I would have remembered by then." He thought about it for a moment, then added, "I'll have to go in to the lab sometime on Sunday, so what do you say we go out to dinner Saturday

115

night? They pull in the sidewalks early here on Sundays."

Julie had hoped to leave Saturday night open just in case Jeff wanted to prolong their date. "I'm going on a picnic that day. I don't know how long it will last but—"

Her mother immediately zeroed in. "What picnic? With whom?"

"With the Ryders, Mother."

"The Ryders?" her mother exclaimed. "Don't tell me that woman is trying to suck you into her family group with all their crazy ideas. I should think you'd have learned your lesson after what her daughter did to you. I'm sure they only want to use you."

"Oh, Mother, this has nothing to do with that or with Mrs. Ryder. It's no big deal. It's just an ordinary picnic with Laura, her brother, and Laura's boyfriend."

"Oh, no big deal? Two boys and two girls? Does that mean you're the brother's date? You've never even mentioned him before."

"Mother, it's not like that!"

"Julie, I wasn't born yesterday. And don't look at me that way. It's not what you think. I know you're old enough to be dating, but according to Noreen Ryder, her boy—and I believe she only has the one—is in college. That's too old for you."

Julie couldn't believe what she was hearing. "He must be all of a year older," she said. "Dad is eight years older than you."

"So he *is* your date?"

"I didn't say that." Her mother always had a way of twisting other people's words. Julie glanced at her father, hoping he would come to her rescue, but he sat, taking in everything and offering nothing.

116

Her mother said, "I wasn't talking about age in years. I mean that college boys are a lot more sophisticated than high school kids, including you. And, another thing, they expect more." The expression on her mother's face told Julie that "more" meant sex.

Her mother continued. "I think you *should* date, Julie, but I just wish you'd pick someone more suitable."

More suitable. Her mother hadn't even met Jeff, so how could she tell whether he was suitable or not? Julie was beginning to suspect that no matter whom she dated, he would be found wanting.

"It doesn't matter anyhow," her mother went on. "I've made plans for that weekend, complete with airline reservations."

Julie stared at her mother, bewildered. "What do you mean?"

A big smile transformed Anne Peters's face. "I mean, you and I are going to spend a long weekend in New York. You can take a couple of school days off. We'll get in a little shopping, see some friends, and really celebrate your birthday. How does that grab you?"

She acts as if I'm a little girl and she's handing me a special treat, Julie thought. She took a deep breath to steady herself, then said, "Mother, you have no right to go ahead and make plans for me without asking if I have any plans of my own." Dr. Almquist would have been proud of me, she thought.

Her father said to her mother, "You never mentioned anything to me."

"I know you. If I'd told you, you would have let something slip. I wanted to surprise Julie."

"Mother, I don't want any surprises!" Julie exclaimed.

"Oh, Julie, come on now, don't disappoint me. I've been

117

looking forward to this ever since we've been out here. We can even take in a show. Besides, you'll be disappointing someone else, too."

Julie glanced suspiciously at her mother. "Who?"

"Well, I wasn't supposed to mention it, but I talked to Morgan this morning, and she just might have a little birthday surprise of her own for you."

"I told you, I don't want surprises."

"Not even something like a little get-together with some of the people you've worked with?"

Before Julie could answer, her father said, "Well, this is all news to me, but in spite of that, I think it's a great idea." He glanced meaningfully at Julie, the way he always did when he wanted her to mollify her mother. "You know how much your mother misses New York. This is a wonderful chance for you two girls to take advantage of the lures of the big city and have yourselves a time."

"Just think of the fun we can have." Her mother went on and on enthusiastically. "You can get together with your friends here any old time."

Julie knew that, in the end, she would give in to her mother's wishes. Hadn't she always? Better to give in on the little things rather than the big, she kept telling herself these days.

The thought crossed her mind that her mother hadn't said one word about the New York trip until Julie had mentioned the picnic. Then she dismissed the suspicion, feeling ungrateful that she hadn't accepted the surprise with better grace. She thought of Jeff, her driver's license, and the picnic— "little" things, surely. Yet why did she feel again that old, familiar ache deep inside her?

118

13

Morgan's apartment was all white, black, silver, and glass, decorated to give a feeling of opulence that awed every new girl she took under her wing. Julie thought it looked more like an unlived-in movie set, but then, Morgan was single, childless, and a perfectionist. Her work was her life, so it was reasonable that, like a magazine picture, the place where she lived should reflect the elegance of a backdrop for some flawlessly beautiful model. Right out of *Vogue*, Julie thought. Unreal.

Morgan, a small brunette with an ageless vitality about her, was saying her good-byes to the last of the people she had invited to Sunday brunch for a visit with Julie. They were a group over whom, Julie knew, Morgan wielded power: a few photographers she'd helped get started and the models known as "Morgan's girls." All she'd had to do was give each of them a call, on the shortest of notice, and say, "You must come to brunch tomorrow. Julie Peters is in town," and not one would dare refuse. Morgan's displeasure was more deadly than the Lord's.

119

They were all here for Morgan, not for me, Julie thought, as she sat on a white, squashy divan, waiting for her mother, who was freshening up in the powder room. Morgan had asked her to remain for a private chat. "You're only going to be here for a week," she'd said. "I know I won't get another chance to talk to you."

Julie glanced out a large picture window that framed an impressive view of the city. A light rain was starting to fall. What would the weather be like in Santa Delores? she wondered. Sunny, probably. A good day for a picnic?

She thought again about Jeff and about how brusquely he had taken her apology. "My mother has already made plans for us to go to New York that weekend," she'd said at their next lesson. "I'm sorry. I didn't know. I'd hoped to try for my license then, and I was really looking forward to a picnic. Do you suppose we can do it when I get back?"

She couldn't tell whether he looked disappointed or relieved. "Oh, sure," he said, shrugging. "Sure. We'll go down to DMV some afternoon and give it a try. I'm sure you'll pass. I think you're ready *now*."

"What about the picnic?"

"Oh, that—well, to tell you the truth, it wasn't any big deal anyhow. And the way it was developing, it was turning into more of a family affair. I'm sure you don't need that."

Perhaps it *was* relief she'd seen in his eyes. He undoubtedly assumed she would be out of place on an outing with his family. Why? Because she was Julie Peters, a creature from a fantasy world who could never quite fit in with real people? "Maybe we could still celebrate if I pass. I mean, maybe we could have our own picnic or something," she ventured, testing her theory.

120

"Maybe," he'd said, a decided note of doubt in his voice. "Of course, I have a pretty busy schedule."

And, with that, they had dropped the subject and everything had gone back to the same cool, businesslike atmosphere that had existed between them before.

Morgan's voice brought her back to the present. "They all thought you were looking wonderful," she said as she strode back into the living room, obviously talking about her departed guests. She settled in a chair across from Julie and studied her. "You *do* look wonderful," she said, "but I think, kiddo, you've taken on a little extra poundage that you could do without. Am I right?"

Of course she was right. All of Morgan's models kept themselves about five pounds underweight, and Julie had been gaining back that crucial five pounds. In answer to Morgan's question, Julie merely shrugged. Morgan, whose wardrobe came out of designers' petites and who constantly dieted to overcome a tendency toward plumpness, couldn't have been more unlike her high-fashion clients, Julie thought.

"Oh, well," Morgan said, "a few pounds isn't all that hard to take off with a little discipline. Make sure you don't let it get out of hand though." She sat back in her chair and gave Julie a look of motherly approval now. "Did I ever tell you that you were the most beautiful child I've ever seen?"

Many times, Julie thought. Instead of answering, she gave what she hoped passed for an appreciative smile.

Morgan smiled back at her. "How have you been, kiddo? Missed the Big Apple?"

"Not really. I've had too many other things to think about."

"I'll bet you have. And, believe me, no one's earned a rest more than you. We were working you too hard—much

121

too hard. Well, there'll be no more of that. From now on, we'll pace you differently."

From now on. "What do you mean?"

"I mean, kiddo, that we'll pick and choose assignments and give you breathing space in between. This summer, for instance—the trip to Scotland will be more like a vacation than work."

Startled, Julie said, "Trip to Scotland?"

"You know—the Jordan St. John collection. He's a marvelous newcomer. Designs clothes to die for. They'll be shooting mostly outdoors, I understand, with old castles in the background. It'll be a lot of fun."

Julie stiffened. "Does my mother know?"

"Of course." When Morgan saw the look on Julie's face, she said, "Didn't she tell you?"

Julie shook her head.

"Whoops! There I go, letting the cat out of the bag. I'll bet she was saving it for a surprise."

I'll bet she was, too, Julie thought. Why am I such an ingrate? I know she's only thinking of my own good. I know she feels that if I give it all up now, someday I'll be sorry. And she's probably right. After all, as she's always telling me, she's lived longer and knows more about the world than I do.

Then why do I resent it so?

Later, when they had returned to their own apartment, she broached the subject with her mother. Anne Peters gave an impishly guilty smile and said, "Darn that Morgan anyhow. *I* wanted to be the one to surprise you. But isn't it great? Maybe we'll be able to talk your father into coming along. He could use a vacation."

"Mother, I don't even know if I'll be ready to go back to

work by this summer." She realized that she was still resorting to the excuse of relapsing into her breakdown, but that seemed to be her only defense when she felt pushed into a corner.

"Oh, don't be so negative. Of course you'll be ready. You've been doing so well lately. Besides, in this kind of business, you can't afford to be away for any great length of time. Morgan figures she can fit you into a spot here and there—nothing taxing—just enough to keep your face before the public."

"But I'll be in school."

"Well, for now, of course. But you'll have holidays and vacations. It will be a good change of scene for you."

Julie sighed. It was always so much easier to go along with her mother's wishes than to fight. She thought of Dr. Almquist. "You have to consider your own needs," he would have said—but he'd never had to stand up to her mother.

That weekend passed uneventfully for Jeff. He caught up on his studying, worked at the Bagel Machine, and puttered with the Mustang. When his mother asked, "What happened to all those plans for a picnic?" he said, "The idea was for a celebration. Now there's nothing to celebrate. Julie's in New York, so she won't be able to take her driving test until she comes back."

"For pity's sake, I don't see why we have to have a reason for a little get-together," his mother said, then appealed to Laura. "How about you?"

Laura looked at her as if she'd never heard the word *picnic*. "It would have been fun, but honestly, Mom, I would have had too much to do anyhow." She went on to enumerate the many obligations that were demanding her time.

When she finished, Jeff added, "It wasn't a very good idea anyhow. I don't have much free time either."

Noreen Ryder gave them both a hurt look. "I'm beginning to think your old Mom isn't good enough for you anymore."

Jeff and Laura had both gone overboard to assure her that that was not the case, and in the end, to mollify her, Jeff had accompanied her to a little theater production of *Sweet Bird of Youth*. Oh, well, he told himself, that was the least he could do for her.

He thought about Julie, hating to admit how disappointed he'd been when she'd told him she was spending the weekend in New York. The news was like a slap in the face. He asked himself if the trip was really necessary or merely a way of making herself unavailable. Of course there would be other weekends for picnics, but maybe she was trying to tell him something. Maybe she thought he was coming on to her too strong. Well, she needn't have worried. Just because she *was* who she was didn't make her that desirable to every guy she met.

Still, she *had* suggested they celebrate together later. . . .

He gave himself a mental kick and determined to put her out of his mind, only to find that, even with his busy life, thoughts of her came stealing back all too often. He decided there was only one thing to do—get the driving test behind them. Then there would be no reason to see each other again.

Although he kept busy, the time dragged. On the night that his mother did her volunteer stint at the ARS office, her car was in the local garage overnight for repairs, so Jeff offered to drop her off on his way to work.

"Calvin Wallace is picking me up," she said. "I thought my sick car would give me an out tonight, but Cal says they have an important newsletter to get out. You could pick me up later though."

"Why? Won't Cal give you a lift home?"

She hesitated for a moment, then said, "Well, to tell you the truth, I don't want him to. I think he's interested in me—well, romantically—and I don't want to encourage him."

Jeff stared at her in surprise. Somehow the idea that his mother might attract a man romantically had never occurred to him. Yet, why not? She was still a good-looking woman. And, all things considered, a guy like Cal should suit her well. "Don't you like him?"

"Of course I like him," she said impatiently. "I'm just not in the market. Your father was all the man I'll ever need—in this lifetime or the next. Besides, I have you kids to think about."

Without knowing why, Jeff felt angry. "We're not kids anymore, Mom!"

Noreen rolled her eyes. "That's what you think."

Sometimes he felt that if anyone was the kid, it was his mother. When Cal arrived, Jeff answered the door and found himself viewing the man in a new light. "Mom will be ready in a minute," he said.

Cal said, "No hurry. Besides, I've been wanting to ask you about that lab job. How soon before they'll be using you?"

"A couple of weeks, according to what they told me."

"Good." Cal's face took on a concerned expression. "We can hardly wait to get our spy into that place."

Jeff felt a sinking feeling in the pit of his stomach. Maybe it was simply the idea of thinking of himself as a spy. Or maybe it was a premonition of something worse to come.

14

"I passed. Can you believe it? I passed!"

For a moment Jeff almost thought Julie was going to throw her arms around him in childlike abandon—and he had to admit he wouldn't have minded—but she seemed to think better of the idea. Instead, as they pulled away from the Department of Motor Vehicles, Julie driving, she went on and on, recounting every small detail of the test. He had never seen her so animated. Her cheeks glowed with color and her eyes sparkled with excitement.

"I was scared to death when I had to parallel park," she said, "but you would have been proud of me, Jeff. I did it perfectly. And I got a hundred on the written—not one mistake!"

"That's great." Jeff had paced up and down the street, waiting nervously, all the time she'd been out with the examiner. When she'd returned with the look of success written all over her face, he'd felt a great sense of relief. But the feeling was short-lived. He was only now beginning to take in the fact that he would have no excuse to see her again.

As she headed the car back toward his house, he said, "You know, even though you're a licensed driver now, you *should* keep your hand in. If you don't drive, you'll lose your confidence."

"I've been thinking about that. If I tell my parents that I want a car, they'll give me a thousand reasons why I shouldn't have one. The only way I'm going to get a car of my own is to just go ahead and get one and not say a word about it. My mother will have a fit, I know, but"—she chuckled—"I'll tell her I wanted to surprise her."

The idea seemed to give her some strange satisfaction that made Jeff wonder. "Cars cost money," he said. "How could you keep something like that from your parents?"

"Easy. I have a checking account of my own—an interest account. My mother opened it for me as a present when I turned sixteen. She said she wanted me to feel that I could buy things on my own if I felt like it. So far, all it's done is collect interest."

Jeff thought she was being naive. "Cars not only cost money, they cost quite a lot of money."

"Oh, I wasn't thinking of a new car. I couldn't afford that out of my checking account. I was thinking of something used, just for driving around town."

"How much can you afford to spend?"

"Do you think I could get something decent for under five thousand dollars? I wouldn't want to clean out the whole account."

In Jeff's experience, people didn't keep that much money in checking accounts. He was reminded again that Julie came from a different world from his. "You should be able to find something clean and reliable for that much. I bought the Mustang used and it's been a great car."

127

"Where did you find it?"

"At Wallace Ford. Cal Wallace, the owner, was a friend of my father's. I told him what I wanted, and when he took this one in on trade, he called me and said he'd found my car. If you want, I could ask him if he can find something for you."

"Oh, would you? That would be perfect. I was wondering where to start looking. I don't know the first thing about cars."

How well Jeff knew. "We could take a run over there now and see what he's got to offer, if you like."

"I'd love to." Then as an afterthought, she added, "I'll pay for the extra time you're putting in."

Embarrassed, Jeff said, "That's not necessary. From now on, it's on the house. Consider it all part of a package deal."

"But that wasn't our agreement."

"Sure it was. Didn't I tell you?"

For a moment she looked doubtful. Then she smiled and gave a helpless shrug. "Okay. If you say so."

Thank God that's settled, Jeff thought. He couldn't stand the idea of taking another cent from her.

They spent the rest of the afternoon visiting the Ford agency where they told Cal Wallace exactly what Julie was looking for. Cal said, "Take a look at what we've got on the used-car lot while I go through the paperwork on our pending deals to see what we've got coming in on trade."

They examined each car on the lot but nothing seemed quite suitable. Finally Cal joined them and said to Julie, "We're taking in a white three-year-old EXP next week—stick shift, sun roof, low mileage—a real cream puff—and the price is well within your budget."

"What's an EXP?" Julie asked.

Jeff said, "It's a small two-seater, just about right for the kind of driving you'll be doing."

Julie said, "Sounds good. When can I see it?"

Cal said, "I'll give you a call when it comes in, Jeff. You can both come down and look it over.

"Do you mind?" Julie asked Jeff.

"Of course not. It's part of our package deal—remember?"

Julie smiled. "I don't know how I'll wait until next week."

They both thanked Cal and set out for Jeff's house, Julie still driving to get in every last moment of practice. Before they reached their destination, she said, "I don't suppose you'll be able to find time for that celebration we were going to have. I mean, it's all right if you can't make it."

He stared at her, at a loss. Did she want to go out with him or was this her way of gracefully getting them both off the hook? Probably the latter. The thought made him feel perverse. He decided to call her bluff. "Sure I can make it. If you still want to try for that picnic, I'll have this Saturday off."

He expected her to make all sorts of excuses. Instead, he was surprised and pleased when she said, "Good. What time?"

"How about if I pick you up around eleven in the morning?" When she agreed, he decided to test her further. "I just remembered—Laura won't be able to make it. She and Brian have other plans," he lied.

A heavy silence fell. At length, she said, "Would you rather do it some other time then?"

"No. It doesn't make any difference to me. I just thought that maybe you'd rather wait until they were available."

She gave an indifferent toss of her head. "It doesn't make any difference to me, either."

"Then maybe we should just go ahead and make it Saturday. After all, celebrations lose their meaning if you wait too long." He thought of his mother and how she would feel if she found out. "Don't say anything to Laura, or she'll talk you into postponing it until she's available. I'll tell her later." He didn't mention that if Laura knew, his mother might well find out and invite herself along.

"I won't say a word," Julie said. "And I'll bring the food."

That was a relief. He had been wondering how he could arrange packing a lunch without giving away his plans.

While he was busy with his thoughts, Julie added, "You don't have to worry about what I'll bring. I'll tell our cook that you're a vegetarian."

"Thanks," he said and flushed at the mention of a cook, again reminded of the chasm between them. Then he pushed the thought away. After all, he'd given her a chance to back out, and she hadn't. "Okay then, it's a date," he said, hoping he was making it perfectly clear that that was exactly what it would be.

"Right," she said, and smiled her beautiful cover-girl smile. Wowee!

15

As far as Julie was concerned, Saturday was the perfect choice of a day for the picnic. By midmorning her mother was out shopping and her father off to the university where he would work until late afternoon. She had the freedom to plan a lunch without a lot of questions and disapproving remarks.

Georgette, challenged by the idea of vegetarian cuisine, rose to the occasion. She prepared three salads, one of vari-colored corkscrew pasta, another of fresh fruit, and a third of uncooked peas and peanuts, a combination that sounded strange but tasted delicious. Julie packed the food away in a well-equipped but never-used picnic basket that sat on a top shelf of the well-stocked walk-in pantry. She added a generous number of Georgette's homemade croissants along with slices of her chocolate torte, a cake layered with rasp-berry and other secret fillings, and covered with a rich, dark icing. Then Julie filled a large thermos with chilled sparkling cider, a substitute for champagne to toast her enormous accomplishment. Getting a driver's license was the first thing she had ever really done on her own. The thought gave her a heady, independent feeling.

When she had packed everything to her satisfaction, she penned a note to her mother:

Mother,

On the spur of the moment, we [she left it to her mother to decide who "we" might be] *decided to have the picnic I told you about before the New York trip. Hope you don't mind. Be home sometime this afternoon.*

Julie

Of course her mother would mind. In fact, she'd be furious, but Julie was determined to enjoy herself anyhow and face the music later.

When Jeff pulled into the circular driveway, she was already outside, waiting. As he loaded the basket into the trunk of his car, she noticed that he glanced toward the house as if expecting her parents to appear. "I'd introduce you to my mother and father," she said, "but they're out."

He grinned. "I can't say I'm sorry I won't be getting the once-over. That's always an ordeal."

As he pulled out of the driveway and headed toward the highway, he said, "I'd let you drive except that we're not going far."

"Oh?"

"I know a place on the way where we can rent bicycles. I thought we'd leave the car there and pedal out to the creek to work up an appetite. How does that sound?"

Julie wasn't sure. "I haven't been on a bicycle since I was a little kid—and then, not often. I don't know if I can ride one anymore."

132

"Don't worry about it. That's something you never forget."

As it turned out, he was right. Julie soon found her balance. Traffic on the road was light, so she didn't have to worry about constantly dodging cars, and she was soon pedaling along with restored confidence. Jeff, wearing a backpack containing his contribution to the affair, rode behind to keep an eye on her, the picnic basket secured to a carrier on his bicycle. The extra weight seemed to give him no problem.

The trip, a distance of about six miles, seemed a long one to Julie. When they arrived at the creek, she was out of breath and hungry. Jeff found a shady clearing under cottonwood and eucalyptus trees to spread the blanket he'd had the foresight to pack, while Julie laid out the red-and-white checked tablecloth that came with the basket.

"Pretty fancy," Jeff said.

"I guess you'd call it a picnic kit—everything we'll need, I hope. It was a Christmas gift from my grandparents back East. I didn't think we'd ever have an occasion to use it."

"Why not?"

"Oh, because my family doesn't usually do things like that. My mother thinks that most picnic spots are too public."

"This one isn't." Jeff took a seat on the blanket, stretched out his long legs, and leaned back on his elbows to watch Julie set out dishes, napkins, and flatware. "Can I help?"

"There's really nothing to do. Georgette—that's our cook—seems to have thought of everything. I hope you like the food."

Apparently he did. He ate as only the overly thin can eat, consuming extra helpings of each of the salads, along with three croissants, and topping off the lunch with the rich torte.

Julie served the cider in plastic glasses with which they toasted her new driver's license, her future car, the warm sunny day, and everything else they could think of.

She found him surprisingly easy to be around. In fact, everything about the day seemed perfect. A warm breeze rippled the creek and made it sparkle in the sunlight. The air was fragrant with the scent of eucalyptus.

"Here's to Georgette, a jewel among cooks," Jeff said, and once more, they touched plastic glasses.

"To Georgette," Julie echoed.

"And last but not least, here's to us, two absolutely terrific human beings." He smiled at her in a way that made her feel all goose pimples.

"I'll drink to that," she said, trying to make her voice sound light.

When they had eaten all they wanted, and Jeff had helped Julie pack away the leftovers, he said, "I know people who would kill for a piece of that torte—my sister, for one."

"Take the rest home. I'll tell Georgette how much you liked it. She loves compliments on her cooking about as much as she loves to cook."

"Thanks," Jeff said. "I know how she feels about compliments. I like them too when *I* cook."

Somehow Julie had a hard time imagining Jeff in that role. "Do you mean to say you actually spend time in the kitchen?"

"I not only spend time there, I cook, and very well if I do say so. I learned from my father. He made things my mother wouldn't dream of fooling with—all kinds of breads and pastries."

"My father fools around in the kitchen once in a while, too, but he doesn't make anything that complicated."

134

"Well, Dad just loved a challenge. Nothing was ever too much trouble to try."

"Whenever you mention your father, you make him sound really special."

"He was. He was an idealist—the kind who practiced what he preached. He was quite a guy."

"I feel the same way about my father." She chuckled. "Most of the time, that is."

"What do you mean—most of the time?"

Julie laughed. "Well, sometimes I get so mad at him because he doesn't seem to pay any attention to what's going on in my life. Then I always have to remind myself that he's kind of like the absentminded professor—so wrapped up in his work that he's not even conscious of where he is half the time. He's sweet though. I guess that makes up for it."

"I've seen his name in the class schedule. He's a psychologist, isn't he?"

"Yes. And sometimes it really gets to me, the way he knows everything about what makes the whole human race tick and nothing about the people closest to him. He says that, to fathers, daughters are a race apart." She shook her head but smiled tolerantly. "The truth is, I really admire him. I mean, he's doing work that he wants to do and work that he feels is important. I only hope I can do as well."

Jeff's long arms hugged his knees as he studied her. "Why shouldn't you? You've got four years of college ahead of you. That should give you plenty of time to decide where you belong. You *are* going, aren't you?"

"Oh, yes—if any of them will have me. My mother wants me to go to an eastern college. She'd really have a fit if she knew about some of the places I've applied."

"Like where?"

"Like USC for one."

"Really? You know what that stands for?"

"Sure—University of Southern California."

"Wrong. Californians call it the University of Spoiled Children."

"Oh? Maybe I'd better skip that one then. How about Stanford? I've applied there, too."

"No kidding! I've applied to Stanford, too."

"I thought you were going to Santa Delores."

"Oh, I probably am. It's just that my uncle suggested it last summer when I was working in his law office. He went there himself. He thought there was some chance of my getting a scholarship. I sort of felt I owed it to him to take a stab at it, although I doubt that I'd follow through, even if I had the chance."

"Why not? If you're as interested in law as you seem to be, a school as prestigious as Stanford should give you an advantage if you want to go on to law school."

"I know, but if I stick with the field my dad suggested, maybe someday I can make some impact on the things he wanted to change—the way we treat other species and the way we handle the earth's resources."

"But couldn't you do just as much if you were a lawyer?" Julie asked.

"Well, in a different way, perhaps. I mean, you could always do volunteer work for one of the groups that's involved, the way Cal Wallace does or, even more important, help to get legislation changed."

"That sounds just as good to me. Besides, if you don't give Stanford a try, you'll regret it the rest of your life."

Jeff, a thoughtful look on his face, said, "You know, it's

really weird how your mind can get so locked onto one track that changing direction seems impossible—even unthinkable."

How well she knew.

"But maybe they won't even accept me at Stanford," he said, "and that will be that."

"But what if they do?"

He pondered the question, then said, "What about you? What if you get an acceptance from Stanford? Will you go?"

"I don't know." Julie had also applied to two eastern colleges of her mother's choosing. Stanford and USC, on the west coast, were only wild, rebellious afterthoughts that her parents knew nothing about.

"Tell you what," Jeff said jokingly. "If we both get accepted, I'll go if you will."

Julie had to smile. "That's not the right reason."

"Maybe it is," he said, sounding as if a new thought had just occurred to him. "I get the feeling that you're trying to break out of some kind of mold. I never really thought about it before, but I wonder if I'm not trying to do the same thing."

"How do you mean?"

"Well, for as long as I can remember, I've been locked into a future my dad chose for me. I thought it was okay, because I believe in all the things he believed in, and I always knew my goals were pretty much the same as his. It just never dawned on me until now that maybe I could accomplish just as much in a different way. Talk about not seeing the forest for the trees!" With a spark of humor in his eyes, he added, "You realize, don't you, that you may have just about straightened out my whole life."

137

She knew he was only half serious, yet the way he looked at her made her feel wise and important. "I wish I could do the same for myself."

"No problem. I'll be glad to do as much for you. It's always easier to solve anyone's problems but your own. If I can help, just ask."

"Maybe I will sometime."

"Anytime," he offered generously, with an expression on his face that invited intimacy.

Julie could feel a fine, silky thread linking them at that moment. "I'll remember that," she said. Then she glanced at her watch. "I guess I should be starting back."

Jeff got to his feet and helped her to hers. He stood facing her, staring deeply into her eyes. "Definitely not blue," he said. "Gray with green flecks."

He's going to kiss me, she thought. A host of worries—her inexperience, her awkwardness compared to other girls—immediately raced through her head. And just as quickly vanished when his lips found hers. The act seemed the most natural one in the world, his touch so familiar that they might have known each other forever. When they finally broke, they stared at each other curiously, as if the magic moment had surprised them both with some enormous discovery.

Jeff was the first to get his bearings. "What better way for two absolutely terrific human beings to get to know each other?" he said, smiling mischievously. "You taste even better than that chocolate torte."

The words relaxed a tension between them, and the self-conscious barrier disappeared. "This terrific human being has got to get home," she said. "Come on."

On the way back, Jeff rode behind again, singing some rousing fighting song about stouthearted men that made her feel silly, young, and happy, the proper end to a wonderful day.

Closer to town the traffic picked up, but Julie was so confident of her balance now and in such soaring spirits that she hardly noticed. As she spotted the bicycle shop coming up, she also saw a car on a side road come barreling down toward the crossing she was nearing. Her own speed had picked up because the terrain was downhill now. The car, she was sure, would come plowing through the intersection just as she reached it unless the driver backed off on the gas. But he didn't. He just sped right along, heading for the corner and her.

Julie panicked. Instinctively, she turned her wheels toward the shoulder of the road. In the next instant, her bicycle hurtled across gravel and into a chain-link fence. The force threw Julie to the ground hard. Her face smashed against a metal post. She lay, stunned, the whole world swimming before her eyes.

The next thing she knew, Jeff was kneeling at her side. "Are you all right?" he asked, a concerned look on his face.

Julie shook her head to clear it. "I think so. For a minute though I thought I was going to pass out."

"Maybe you'd better stay where you are. You might have broken something."

Julie tested her right arm and leg where she had hit and scraped along the ground. Both were smarting, but, other than that, seemed to be functional. "Everything seems to be in one piece." She felt her cheekbone and was surprised to find blood on her hand.

"Can you stand up?" Jeff asked.

"I think so." She was still too stunned to feel much of anything as Jeff helped her to her feet.

139

He examined her and said, "You really skinned your hand and arm. That's not as bad as your face though. It's bleeding. You must have really banged yourself."

Julie was starting to become aware that her hand and arm were smarting now. Her leg ached and there was a burning sensation on her cheekbone.

Jeff said, "You were going along so well. What happened?"

"I was afraid he wasn't going to stop at the intersection and was going to hit me." She pointed to the car that had provoked her disastrous reaction. To her great surprise, it had come to a full stop and was now making a right turn around the corner. Julie had never felt more stupid and embarrassed in her life.

Jeff dug a handkerchief out of his jeans pocket and gave it to her to stanch the flow of blood from the gash on her cheek. "I don't like the look of that," he said. "You wait here. I'll return your bicycle and get the car. Then I'm taking you to emergency."

As he hurried off, Julie was more concerned with her stupidity than with her injuries. Dumb, dumb, dumb, she kept telling herself. Then an even worse thought occurred to her. Her mother would find out.

16

"Do you realize what you've done to your face?" Anne Peters paced restively through Julie's bedroom as Julie lay on the bed, stretched out on her back, Daisy curled up on her chest.

Julie's hand immediately went to the bandage that covered her cheek. How scary to think of being disfigured for life! To reassure herself as well as her mother, she said, "The doctor says I shouldn't even have a scar in spite of all the stitches. And he ought to know. He's a plastic surgeon." Although Julie had hit the metal post, her cheek had also scraped against a ragged piece of fencing that had somehow torn loose. The sharp edge had cut the skin, leaving a nasty gash.

"I don't care what that doctor said. What do emergency-room surgeons know? Monday I'm taking you to someone I can really trust."

Julie said nothing. Her mother was obviously very upset. She was always an alarmist when anything occurred that might in some way alter Julie's looks. "This would never

141

have happened if you hadn't tried to deceive me," she said.

"I didn't try to deceive you. I left you a note."

"Yes, and it said nothing about spending the day all alone with that boy."

Because Julie was underage, the emergency-room personnel had insisted on getting a parent's consent before they treated her. Her mother, the only one home at the time, had hurried over to sign the form, obviously against her better judgment. She had yielded only because they told her a plastic surgeon would handle the job. To make matters worse, she'd had to contend with the shock of Jeff's presence as she'd listened in stony silence while he'd explained what had happened.

Julie said now, "Jeff and I were only on a harmless picnic, Mother. The accident was my own fault."

"I just don't understand what's gotten into you since we've come out here. This isn't at all like you, Julie. You should never have let him talk you into riding a bicycle in the first place. You haven't had enough experience on one."

And whose fault is that? Julie thought. Her mother had always treated her like a china doll, too fragile to do anything physically risky.

Her mother said, "Ever since you started going over to the Ryder house I've had a feeling that nothing good would come of it. Now I find it isn't the girl you're interested in; it's the boy."

"Mother, Laura is a friend. I like her. Through her I met Jeff. I like him too. I've never had any friends of my own before. Please don't spoil it for me."

"Oh, Julie . . ." Her mother stopped pacing and perched on the edge of the bed. "I don't want to spoil anything for you, but you can't expect me to feel kindly toward people

I didn't like to begin with, and now that I find they've caused you harm—"

"Mother, I told you it was my own fault. Nobody caused me harm but myself. I did something stupid, and I fell down. It happens to people every day. Next time I'll be more careful. I don't see why you have to make such a big deal over it."

"Next time! There won't *be* any next time." Her tone startled Daisy, who leaped off the bed and disappeared beneath it. "I want you to promise me you won't see this boy again and that you'll stay away from that house."

Julie stiffened and sat up. "That's not fair, Mother. The Ryders had nothing to do with this."

"One of them certainly did. If that boy hadn't put you up to riding a bicycle—"

"Nobody put me up to anything. Don't you understand that I *want* to do things that other people do?"

"No one says you can't, but you don't have to do things that are dangerous. You don't seem to realize, Julie, how special you are." She leaned forward and took Julie's uninjured hand. "Do you have any idea how few girls have the assets that you have? It would be sinful if you didn't take care of them and use them the way God intended."

How could her mother possibly know *what* God intended? Julie's assets also included a good brain, but she knew her mother wasn't talking about that. "Mother, I really think you're overreacting. I didn't even break anything, and the doctor says my face will be all right. As far as Laura and Jeff are concerned, I think you're jumping to conclusions. If I'd picked up with someone who was into drugs or something like that, I could see your point, but they're both about as straight as you can get. They're nice people."

143

"I'm not saying they're not. I just don't like the things that have happened to you since you met them—that episode at school—now this. Besides, you're not confiding in me anymore. I had no idea you knew that boy well enough to date him."

The guilt began to creep in again. Julie had deliberately kept that information and more from her mother. "Well, I do," she said defensively.

A look of anguish passed over her mother's face. "I'm only concerned about you, because I don't want you to get hurt. An ordinary boy like this Jeff could date you for his own reasons. Kids like that feel it gives them prestige to be able to say they dated someone as well known as you."

What her mother didn't seem to realize was that Jeff was no ordinary boy. "Don't worry," she said. "I don't think he'll want to date a klutz like me a second time."

"What I'm hoping is that *you* won't want to date *him* a second time. After all, you're much too young to get serious about anyone. In your position, Julie, when you're ready, you'll be able to have your pick of men."

Julie frowned. "What position is that?"

"Why, as a top model, of course."

"Mother, I am not exactly a top model anymore. I haven't done anything for about a year now. And you know as well as I do that this is a fickle business. Next year no one may want me."

"Of course they'll want you."

"But maybe I won't want them."

Her mother gasped. "Sometimes I get the feeling that you don't appreciate all I've done for you. I don't think you have any concept of how hard I've worked."

"I know how hard you've worked."

"No, you don't know. You don't have the foggiest notion of the time and effort I've put in—even to kissing backsides—just to get you this far."

Julie could see tears gathering in her mother's eyes. "I know—I really do." She wished only that she could feel more gratitude. "Don't let's argue, Mother."

Her mother gave a deep sigh. "You're right. You should be resting." She got off the bed. "I won't say any more. As for that Ryder boy and girl—I suppose you'll do what you want no matter how I feel about it." When Julie failed to respond, she added, "Just don't deceive me—okay?"

Julie nodded. Again she felt guilty about all she had been doing behind her mother's back—the driving lessons, the car. . . . Was she being an unfeeling monster? Perhaps she should forgo the car right now rather than hurt her mother further.

Anne Peters stood up and sighed again. "Believe me, I just can't wait until summer."

Julie, perplexed, asked, "What's summer got to do with anything?"

"Why, the trip to Scotland, of course. A little vacation from this place will give us both a better perspective."

Julie had almost forgotten about the modeling trip to Scotland. With her mother's words, a cold anger swept through her. A moment ago she had considered abandoning the idea of buying a car for herself. Now she knew she had to have one just to make her feel that she had some control over her own life. When her mother left the room, Julie could feel traces of the old fears and anxieties. Then she thought of Jeff's kiss and, slowly, they began to fade.

*　　*　　*

On Thursday after classes, Jeff hurried home, not at all sure he'd find Julie there. He had called her on Sunday only to learn that her mother planned to whisk her off to San Francisco the following day to see some famous plastic surgeon. He immediately assumed there must be something seriously wrong, but Julie assured him that was not the case. Her mother evidently didn't believe that anyone local could be worthwhile. They would probably return by Wednesday night, Julie said.

According to Cal, the trade-in was ready for her now, and Jeff had asked Laura to relay the message to Julie if she was in school that day. He wondered, though, if she would really follow through on the deal. He knew that her parents had not sanctioned the purchase, and after meeting her mother and seeing how she had taken the bicycle accident, he wouldn't have been at all surprised if Julie backed out just to avoid the hassle.

After all, he was very much involved in the whole thing, and it was obvious not only that her mother was shocked to find Julie with some guy she'd hardly even heard of but that she had no intention of giving the relationship her blessing. Jeff had worried about the situation since Saturday. If only he had never mentioned renting bicycles. If only he had gone first on the way back or watched her more carefully. If only . . . The fault was his, he was sure.

Now as he zipped into his driveway, parked, and hurried to the house, he convinced himself that she wouldn't be there, that she blamed him and wanted nothing more to do with him, that he'd never see her again. When he opened the front door and heard her and Laura's voices, he breathed a great sigh of relief.

146

Smiling, his doubts and fears gone now, he strode into the living room where they were apparently waiting for him. Then he took one look at her, and the smile froze on his face. She had a nasty dark bruise all around her eye and a bandage over a swollen cheekbone. "Wow!" he said, feeling guilty again. "For some reason, it never occurred to me you'd have a shiner, too."

To his relief, she laughed. "If you think this is bad, you should have seen it Sunday. My mother thought I should skip school until I looked more human, but I didn't want to."

Laura said, "I'll bet you wished you had after all the ribbing you had to take."

Julie smiled in a way that made Jeff think she had enjoyed the ribbing. Did it take something like this to make her feel she belonged? "What did the San Francisco doctor say?"

"He said that he couldn't have done any better than the doctor here and to leave well enough alone. He didn't think I'd even have a scar."

"Too bad," Laura said. "Scars always make people look more interesting."

"I think so, too," Julie said. "On other people."

Jeff changed the subject. "I guess Laura told you about the car."

"Yes, and I can hardly wait to see it."

"Come on then. I'll drive you." He turned reluctantly to his sister. "Want to come?" As Julie's eyes rested on Laura, waiting for her answer, he signaled Laura with a shake of his head and mouthed the word *no*.

He could tell Laura was suppressing a knowing smile as she said, "Can't. I've got too much to do here. I have to wash my hair and do my nails and feed the cat and—"

147

He didn't wait for what promised to be a long list of invented chores. "Come on then, Julie, let's go."

On the way to the auto dealership, Jeff, hoping to find out where he stood with her, said, "I didn't really expect you to show today."

"I told my mother that Laura was helping me catch up on the work I'd missed at school."

"That's not exactly what I meant. I meant I thought maybe you'd change your mind about things."

Out of the corner of his eye, he saw her glance quickly his way. "What things? The car?"

"Well, yes—that and other things."

"I almost did have second thoughts about the car, but no, I think I need to do this."

"What if you don't like the car or, for some reason, it's just not right?"

"Then I'll wait until there's another one that *is* right." She sounded very determined. "You said *other things* besides the car. What other things?"

He said simply, "Me."

Sounding puzzled, she asked, "How?"

"Oh, I thought maybe you'd feel like suing me or something?"

She glanced at him, a mystified expression on her face. "Why would I sue you?"

"Well, if I hadn't had the bright idea to rent bicycles, and if I'd—"

She broke in. "Why should I blame you because I'm such a klutz?" She chuckled. "Not that I wouldn't love to blame someone else."

Jeff, who'd felt as if he were holding his breath, relaxed

now. "Does that mean we can pick up where we left off?" He took his eyes off the road just long enough to see a small smile form on her lips.

"You mean you're willing to go out with someone who does really dumb things and looks like her head got caught in a Cuisinart?"

He grinned. "Sure. I've got a thing for klutzy girls with shiners."

He was surprised at how shy she sounded as she said, "I guess it would be all right then."

The words made him feel all warm inside. "I don't have to work tomorrow night. How about taking in a movie? There's a theater near the university that's running an Ingmar Bergman classic."

"I'm not sure I understand Ingmar Bergman films."

What was that supposed to mean? Was she backing away now? "I'll educate you," he offered.

He could hear an impish note in her voice as she said, "In that case, I'd love to go."

They exchanged broad smiles then, and Jeff felt there was hope of recapturing the special moment they'd experienced at the picnic.

When they arrived at the Ford dealership, Cal took care of them personally. The car was certainly the cream puff he'd claimed, with gleaming white paint and a smart black interior. Julie walked all around it, patted it, sat in it, and, as far as Jeff was concerned, did everything but hug it. At Cal's insistence, they took it out for a trial run, but, Jeff felt, they were only going through the motions of acting like cautious consumers. Julie's mind was obviously already made up.

149

While Cal took her into his office to take care of the paper-work, Jeff killed time looking over the other cars on the lot. Finally, she emerged from the building, jangling a set of car keys, a triumphant gleam in her eyes. "I just can't believe it," she said. "The only thing I have to worry about is insurance, but I know my dad will take care of that once he knows I have a car."

With a show of gallantry, Jeff opened the door for her. As she slid into the seat, he asked, "Do you want me to follow you home for moral support?"

"That's a tempting offer, but no. I want to see how it feels to perform by myself, without someone waiting in the wings to catch me if I fall."

He had the feeling she was talking about more than driving a car. "How about tomorrow night? Can I pick you up around eight thirty?"

She hesitated. "Is it all right if I call you at home later? I'll know better about the time then."

"Sure," he said, a little disappointed that their date wasn't firmly fixed. "I hope your parents like the car."

She groaned. "It's going to come as one big surprise."

"They'll survive it."

"I just hope I do."

Jeff sensed that selling her parents on the car was not exactly going to be a piece of cake. He waved her off and watched as she left the lot and turned the car in the direction of her home, handling the vehicle with confidence, yet with a beginner's caution. She'd do all right. He felt rather proud of his achievement.

He got into his Mustang and headed home, looking forward to Julie's call that night. No sooner had he walked into the house than Laura said, "There's a message for you from somebody at the university. They want you to start some lab job. I wrote down the particulars."

Jeff frowned. "Did they say when?"

"Tomorrow."

Tomorrow! In other circumstances, Jeff would have felt elated to have the chance to earn extra money. Instead, he felt depressed.

17

"And all the time I thought you were studying with the girl, you were out driving around with that boy. Then you go behind my back and buy a car!" Anne Peters said, shaking her beautifully coiffured head in disbelief as she stood with Julie in the driveway.

"I wasn't going behind your back, Mother, any more than you were going behind mine when you planned that trip to New York." Julie took some satisfaction now in trying to pay her mother back in kind. "You just wanted to surprise me. That's all *I* was doing. I thought you'd be pleased that I was learning how to handle things by myself."

Her mother stared at her for a moment, obviously aware of the significance behind Julie's act yet not willing to acknowledge it. "If you mean that as sarcasm, you surprised me all right, but not happily, I'm sorry to say. Honestly, Julie, did you think I wouldn't approve of your learning to drive?"

That was exactly what Julie thought, but she said nothing, merely shrugged.

"Of course I approve. Everyone should know how to drive. I'd have chosen an accredited driving school to teach you though, not just—just anybody. As for the car, your father and I have been talking about buying a second one. He wants something more sporty for himself. You and I could have shared the Mercedes."

Julie knew what that would have meant. Things would be no different from the way they were now. Her mother would always need the car. Julie would still be dropped off and picked up at school, like a small child. "Well, now we won't have to share," she said.

"If you wanted a car, you could have had a new one. At the very least you might have asked your father for advice instead of going to this boy and taking the first thing some used-car salesman palmed off on you."

Julie explained that Cal Wallace was not a used-car salesman but the owner of the company and a friend of the Ryders who had chosen the car carefully and with her in mind.

"I don't care," her mother said. "What you didn't consider is that your father's feelings will be hurt."

Now Julie could tell her mother was clutching at straws. "Mother, Daddy is the last person to ask about cars, or anything mechanical for that matter. He's always said that that's why he pays other people to advise him." Her mother was obviously feeling not only angry but frustrated. She loved managing Julie's affairs and felt cheated now.

She regarded the car for a long moment, looking disdainful and, at the same time, troubled. Finally, she said, "Julie, come inside. I was having a cup of tea. Join me. We have to talk."

They both went inside to the room her mother had decorated with lots of white wicker and greenery and where her half-full teacup was waiting for her on a glass-topped table. She freshened it with steaming liquid from a silver pot and offered a cup to Julie, who refused. Then she sighed absently and said, "I don't like this place. I don't like this place at all."

Julie had guessed as much but this was the first time her mother had voiced the thought.

Anne Peters continued. "I think the move served a purpose. It's given your father a chance to add to his reputation as a researcher. As for you, you aren't as nervous as you used to be, but I can't say I like what's happening to you otherwise. But that's not the point. What I'm getting at is I'm going to become a basket case if we have to stay here much longer."

Julie regarded her mother with surprise. Why, she looks desperate, Julie thought. She had been so full of her own needs, she had given almost no thought to her mother's. Here was a woman whose life, until now, had been buzzing with activity. She'd been constantly involved in managing Julie's career. There were always other people to talk to, to argue with, to convince. There were contracts to consider and lawyers to consult. Until Julie's illness, her day had hardly given her a moment to breathe. And she'd thrived on it. Now this bright, energetic woman was tucked away in a quiet town with nothing more exciting to tax her talents than decorating the house and hiring help to keep it. Whatever her mother's faults, she had sacrificed her own needs to Julie's and her husband's in coming to Santa Delores.

Anne Peters said, "In spite of what you think about me, I do understand why you wanted to know how to drive and even why you wanted your own car."

154

"You do?" Julie said, a little stunned at the change in her mother's tone.

"Of course I do. When I was your age, I used to be so jealous of the girls in high school who whisked around town in their parent's cars or their own. We couldn't even afford a car."

Her mother seldom talked about her upbringing, Julie thought. Her grandfather had not only divorced her grandmother when Julie's mother was still a baby, but he'd deserted them both. They never saw him again. Julie's grandmother supported herself and her daughter on a modest salary earned by managing a small Lerner's dress shop. If only she'd had more ambition, Julie's mother always said. That was certainly not *her* trouble, Julie decided.

Her mother said wistfully, "I may hate the idea of your driving around alone, exposed to all the dangers out there these days, but I do understand it." She reached across the table, and her hand enclosed Julie's. "Honestly."

Julie stared at her mother, unbelieving. "Somehow I didn't think you would."

"Come on, now. I'm not exactly an ogre. I was your age once, too."

Julie contained a sigh of relief. If her mother was willing to accept the situation, her father would go along with it, too.

Anne Peters drew her hand from Julie's and sipped her tea thoughtfully. "I'm sorry we had to buy here, but there just wasn't anything decent to rent."

"But we did buy and it's all over and done with," Julie said. "Besides, it's a nice house."

Her mother leaned forward, elbow on the table, chin rest-

155

ing on her palm. "That's what I want to talk to you about."

Julie tensed, afraid now of what was coming.

Her mother said, almost as if she were talking to herself, "It can't matter that much to you. You haven't been here very long, and next semester you'll be in college. As for your father, he'll be happy wherever they let him carry on with his work. And he *has* talked about a career change."

Julie opened her mouth to ask what her mother meant, but before she could get out the words, her mother went on, "One thing this move has taught me is that I'll never be happy in a place like this." She reached into the pocket of the jacket she wore, drew out a long envelope, and handed it to Julie. "Open it."

Julie glanced at the letter with mixed emotions. It was from Yale University, one of the colleges to which she'd applied.

"Open it," her mother said again.

Nervously, Julie tore open the envelope to read the message inside. "They've accepted me," she murmured, hardly believing her eyes.

"Oh, I knew it," her mother said. "The minute I saw the envelope, I just knew it. How could they refuse you when you did so well on the S.A.T.s? That's terrific! You couldn't ask for a better school. And you'll be in New Haven, only about two hours from New York. And, come to think of it, your father knows some important people at Yale. That shouldn't hurt you any. Oh, thank God we kept the New York apartment. You must write back right away, Julie."

"I'd rather wait until I've heard from every place I've applied," Julie said. She had to admit it was a great honor to be accepted into Yale, but having her mother close enough to keep on running her life—and she was sure that would be the case—took the thrill out of it. Besides, wasn't college supposed to mean being on your own? How could she give up that idea? And what about her relationship with Jeff?

The thought of Jeff reminded her of their date for tomorrow night. She had put him off deliberately, afraid her mother would find some reason to keep her from going out with him. Now, no matter what, she decided to take a firm stand. "Mother, I'm going to a movie with Jeff tomorrow night. He wants to pick me up at eight thirty. Is that all right with you?" She waited, poised for an argument.

Much to her surprise, her mother said absently, "Jeff? Oh, the Ryder boy. Yes, I guess eight thirty will be all right. Just make sure he comes into the house. Your father will want to meet him."

Now that her mother was picturing Julie at Yale, far, far from Santa Delores, she could afford to be generous.

18

"They should have started you a week ago. Lord knows I gave them enough notice." Bob Sanders, the senior whose job Jeff was taking over, opened the door of the seedy-looking cinderblock building that housed the labs. He and Jeff passed under a sign that read, "No Admittance to Unauthorized Personnel." "But, no, they're so afraid of spending an extra dime," Bob continued. "As it is, I've had to come in on my own time just to show you the ropes."

"Sorry if it's putting you out," Jeff said.

"Oh, that's okay. Won't take long. There's never anyone around to get in your way this early in the morning."

As Jeff stepped into what Bob told him was the medical lab, the heavy stench of urine accosted his nostrils. He must have unconsciously made a face, because Bob said, "You'll get used to the stink."

Jeff didn't think so, and he was glad he wouldn't be around long enough to try. The next thing he noticed was that although there were unmistakable dog and cat sounds, there was none of the lively barking and caterwauling you expected from healthy animals.

Bob led Jeff through the lab, showing him where the food was kept and giving him instructions on feeding and watering the many dogs, cats, rabbits, guinea pigs, and rodents that were penned there.

Jeff stared in amazement at the deplorable conditions that surrounded him. In spite of whatever the ARS had heard, he had never expected anything quite this bad. Dogs stood in their own urine on bare cement floors. A lone bloodhound covered with a bloody discharge lay in a barren, damp enclosure next to newborn pups, some obviously dead, the others probably dying. Cats were caged with no litter pans, fecal matter accumulating beside their water bowls. The place was a filthy mess with junk piled high atop shoddy cages, broken floor tiles preventing proper sanitation, and, with all that, wiring and insulation that was falling from the ceiling.

"Why doesn't somebody clean this place up?" Jeff said, not trying to hide his disgust and concern.

Bob shrugged. "Don't worry about it. They can't expect you to do it—not on what they're paying. Besides, there's enough to do. You'd never have the time. I told them they'd have to hire someone full-time if they expected the messes cleaned up too."

Jeff noticed a cage with three cats with wires implanted in their skulls. "What's that all about?" he asked.

"Something to do with studying Sudden Infant Death Syndrome."

"How can they study that in cats? From everything I've read it only happens in people."

"Search me. I imagine they know what they're doing though."

159

Jeff wasn't so sure. He noticed a mixed retriever lying in a pen, its right eye sewn shut, its throat draining pus. The animal looked completely debilitated. "What are they supposed to be studying with this guy?"

"Look, I don't keep up on everything they're doing here. If you're interested, you can check the files." He pointed to several cabinets along the wall. "They document everything."

The ARS would be glad to hear that, Jeff thought.

In a voice that attempted to sound sympathetic, Bob said, "It seems a bit much at first, but you'll get used to it. Just tell yourself that it's all in a good cause." He took Jeff by the arm. "Come on. I'll show you the psych lab now. It's right through that door." He fished a key from his pocket, unlocked the door, then handed the key to Jeff. "That's yours now. It works for both labs. If you think what you've seen here is bad, you should see the creepy stuff the psych profs have going."

Inside the psychology lab, Jeff immediately noticed the large number of monkeys used there and asked about them.

"I guess researchers think they respond more like people," Bob said. "Take these, for instance." He indicated what must have been more than fifty rhesus monkeys housed in small cubicles. They all had tubes implanted in their arms and were behaving like no monkeys that Jeff had ever seen before. One of them seemed to be plucking hairs out of his arms. Another looked as if he was trying to bite off his toes. Another was obviously dead.

Jeff asked, "What's wrong with them?"

"They're stoned out of their minds, that's what. Some of them are given cocaine, some morphine—all kinds of different drugs. All they have to do is press a lever that controls the intake in those tubes, and they can have all they want."

"Until it kills them?"

Bob glanced at the dead monkey. "Yeah, some of them. They finally get convulsions and die. And that reminds me— don't forget to have me show you what to do with the guys that made it to vivisection heaven." He chuckled. "I figure they've earned heaven after they've been through this place."

All Jeff could think of was how often, in speeches to interested groups, he'd heard his dad quote the French physiologist Claude Bernard who stated that a member of *his* profession was not an ordinary man. ". . . He is a scientist, possessed and absorbed by the scientific idea that he pursues," Bernard had said back in the last century. "He does not hear the cries of animals, he does not see their flowing blood, he sees nothing but his idea, and is aware of nothing but an organism that conceals from him the problem he is seeking to resolve." Then Jeff's father would add, "Bernard, the experimenter, was giving us a self-portrait. He was talking about a man who had done a psychological vivisection on himself and had turned into a subhuman."

Bob interrupted Jeff's thoughts, gesturing to follow him over to a cage on the other side of the room. "Here's one for the books." He pointed to a baby monkey, clinging to what looked like a cloth replica of a larger monkey. "This is what I call the monster mother. Watch."

As they both stood, observing the tiny animal, suddenly a sharp wire frame embedded in the cloth body shot forward with a force that ejected the baby monkey and tossed it to the floor where it lay stunned. After a long moment, the infant, pathetic and empty-eyed, picked itself up, waited

161

until the wire returned into the cloth body, then dragged itself back to cling again to the hostile surrogate mother and wait to be rejected still another time.

Bob pointed to several cages behind the one they were looking at. "There are five other monkeys in the experiment. They were taken from their mothers at birth," he explained. "As I understand it, what we're trying for here is to see how long it takes to turn them into psychos. I can't say I really understand the purpose, but then, what do I know?"

"Weird," Jeff said.

Bob went to the file cabinet, pulled out some papers, and handed them to Jeff. "If we're talking weird, read that."

Jeff glanced at the researcher's notes, which talked about trying to induce depression in the monkeys. It seemed he and his aides had first tried high-pressure air in the cloth mother. "It just about blew the skin off the baby but did not serve the purpose of achieving psychopathology, because the baby only clung tighter to the mother," the paper said, and concluded, "Apparently a frightened infant will cling to its mother at all costs."

With the next try, Jeff read, they had built a surrogate that rocked so violently that the baby's head and teeth rattled. Still unsatisfied, they'd tried the current step with the embedded wire. Even now, the results hadn't suited them. Hastily penciled notes indicated new and, to Jeff, just as sick plans ahead.

In fact, as far as he was concerned, the whole experiment sounded not only stupid but worthless, probably existing for no other reason than for some professor to write and publish just one more useless paper. "You wonder what kind of a guy it takes to dream up something like this," he said, his

162

revulsion growing by the minute. He handed the papers back to Bob, who replaced them in the files.

"A new guy—Professor Peters," Bob said. "He's doing a lot of work in psychopathology. I told you you'd find a lot of kinky things going on here."

Jeff nodded. He no longer trusted himself to comment. Then as he followed Bob around the lab, the significance of what he'd heard suddenly hit him. Peters! Oh, my God, Julie's father! And when Jeff passed on his new information to the ARS, they would raid the place, taking with them the files that gave explicit documentation about each experiment and everyone connected with it. Through other organizations that protected them, they would also make sure that newspapers got the full story, complete with photos taken by the raiders and names of professors guiding the work. Certainly no one would spare Julie's father.

What would happen if her father was held up to public ridicule and disdain for initiating a project that seemed cruel and senseless? Julie could very easily put two and two together and blame Jeff. She obviously thought the world of her father. You could tell by the way she talked about him. And yet, how could she respect the man, knowing he was involved in something so monstrous? Until now, Jeff had believed that she'd shared his concern for animals, had understood and sympathized with the ARS and its objectives. Was he wrong? Or was it possible that she knew nothing about her father's experiments?

Sickened by everything he'd seen, he was more than ready to follow through on the plan he and Cal had concocted. He had to get a duplicate key on his lunch hour, then turn the original back to Bob that very day, saying he wouldn't be

163

able to to handle the work, that he'd just talked to his boss on his other part-time job, and the man wanted him to put in more hours. That way, the ARS insisted, no one could connect him to anything that happened. After that, it was entirely up to them.

Oh, yes, he knew what was expected of him, but thinking about how much he could hurt Julie made him feel every bit as sick as his visit to the lab. He just didn't see how he could do this to her.

"What did you think of the flick?" Jeff asked Julie as they drank Cokes at a coffee shop near the theater. All evening disturbing thoughts of the lab had filled his mind, coming between them, casting a shadow over a date he'd had such high hopes for.

If Julie sensed anything wrong, she never showed it. "I thought the movie was—well, interesting."

"Only interesting?" He had no reason to challenge her, but he felt perverse, almost as if she were responsible for the existence of that whole filthy laboratory.

"To tell you the truth, I had the feeling there was all kinds of symbolism I was missing."

He immediately enlightened her with a detailed explanation that went on a mite too long in a voice a shade too superior.

When he finished, she said agreeably, "I'm really impressed. I would never have seen all that in it if you hadn't told me."

After his arrogance, her good-natured reply came like a slap in the face. You hypocritical smartass, he chided himself, then said with more humility, "I would never have seen that much in it either, if I hadn't read the reviews."

She laughed, and he gave a wry smile which was the best he could manage under the circumstances. Although he'd tried, he just couldn't put out of his mind his doubts about her. He was sure she had to know something about her father's lab work, yet if that were the case, you'd have thought she'd have taken issue with him and Laura when they'd made it clear they were confirmed antivivisectionists.

To add to his anguish, he had met her father now, and the man seemed like a decent enough guy in spite of his morbid experiment. In fact, he'd acted a lot more pleasant than his wife, thanking Jeff for teaching Julie to drive and helping her find a car. Of course there had been the usual cross-examination about Jeff's college courses, his teachers, his major, the movie they were seeing, the location of the theater, all couched in a jovial and interested manner that softened the customary parental third-degree.

On the other hand, Julie's mother had civil inquiries about his mother and his sister, and, all the while, Jeff had the feeling that she couldn't have been less interested. Her significant contribution to the conversation came as he and Julie were about to leave. "The movie's over at eleven fifteen"— she'd obviously looked it up—"so we'll expect you home about eleven thirty, Julie," she'd said.

Jeff had quickly put in, "If Julie feels like it, I thought we'd stop for something to eat."

The expression on Anne Peters's face told Jeff she didn't think much of that idea. "Well, why don't you come along home and have something here. At least it won't be junk food."

"Oh, Mother," Julie said, sounding embarrassed, "we'll be home when we get here."

Her mother shot Julie's father a look that was about as

165

subtle as an elbow jab, and he immediately said, "Well, just don't be too late." Then he turned to Jeff and added, "Take good care of our girl."

Jeff had assured him he would, and when he and Julie were outside, she'd apologized and tried to pass off their concern with "They're a couple of mother hens."

Indeed they were. Their message had come through loud and clear. *Don't mess with our daughter or you'll have to answer to us.* Jeff always expected a little of that kind of treatment when he dated a girl, but he sensed their concern was almost neurotic.

As if he hadn't had enough on his mind that day, when he'd arrived home in the afternoon, he'd found a long white envelope from Stanford in the mailbox. Forcing himself to remain calm, he'd opened it and glanced at the letter inside. With almost a feeling of shock, he realized they had accepted him. He had not expected to feel excited by the idea, but he did.

He glanced over to Julie now, noticing that the swelling around her eye had gone down although she still wore a bandage over the wound. If she had ever seemed intimidating to him, the knowledge that she could bleed as readily as other people helped minimize the picture of an invincible magazine cover. He found himself saying, "I had an acceptance from Stanford today."

Her face lit up as she exclaimed, "How wonderful! Does your mother know?"

"No. I haven't even told Laura. Lucky she wasn't home when the mail came or she'd have blabbed it all over."

"When *are* you going to tell them?"

"I don't know. I want to talk to my uncle first."

"About the scholarship?"

166

"Among other things. But he did say he couldn't do anything about it unless or until I was accepted. It's through a lawyers' club he belongs to. They're all Stanford grads."

"Well now you've been accepted."

"It's just not that easy a decision to make. It seems foolish to change schools when I can stay at Santa Delores and get my bachelor's. I can still go on to law school."

"Sounds like you're doing a good job of talking yourself out of it."

"I suppose I am. What about you? Have you heard from any of the colleges you've applied to?"

She nodded. "You're not the only one who's had an acceptance. Yale seems to want me."

Yale! His hand tightened on his glass. That would put her clear across the continent. Then he told himself that was probably just as well. He had the power to damage her father's work—even his reputation—and, in the process, hurt her. If he decided to use that power, there was no way they could even end up as friends, let alone anything else. "Are you going?"

"I don't know. Like you, I haven't decided yet."

She'd go, Jeff was sure. Yale was too good to turn down. Imagining her forever out of his life, a kind of bittersweet longing came over him, an ache for the might-have-been. He wanted to reach out and touch her, to feel the softness of her lips against his again. "You'd be a long way from your family," he said softly.

She sighed. "Not really. My mother has it all figured out that she'll stay in the New York apartment, and we'll still be"—a shadow crossed her face—"well, together. I don't know what she has in mind for Dad, but I'm sure she'll convince him he belongs back there too."

167

She obviously didn't like the idea. Did that mean she might reconsider? He said without thinking, "What about your father's work—his research?"

"Oh, did I tell you about that?" she said.

Jeff tensed. Then she did know! And he'd had every intention of being a nice guy tonight and not mentioning a word about the lab and what went on there. Now he couldn't restrain himself. The thing that had been eating away at him all day came spilling out. "You mean you know what he's doing, and it doesn't bother you?"

For a moment she looked bewildered. "Why should it bother me?"

"Because it's cruel, and it's stupid." He saw her stiffen and immediately regretted the words. Not that they didn't need saying, but he could have been more diplomatic.

"What are you talking about?"

Why was she acting so innocent? "You know what he's working on, don't you?"

"Well, of course I know. He's doing research in psychopathology. Naturally I don't know all the details. He never talks much about his work until he's published his conclusions."

"How do you justify what he's doing to those poor monkeys?"

"What monkeys?"

She didn't know! Jeff mentally groaned, wishing now that he'd never broached the subject. "I'm sorry. I shouldn't have said anything."

"But you did, so I think you'd better go on."

"I'd rather you asked your father."

"Maybe I will, but right now, I'm asking you."

The stubborn set of her chin suggested a Julie he had not

known existed. She was a person who would go to great lengths to stand up for someone she loved, a quality he would have admired at any other time. "I don't think I should get into this," he said. "I'm sorry I brought it up in the first place."

She gave an impatient gasp. "Look, you've as good as called my father cruel and stupid. I think you owe me an explanation."

There was no way he could squirm out of talking about it now. Then it occurred to him that maybe she'd understand his feelings better if she heard the story. He took a deep breath and began describing her father's experiment in the straight forward, unemotional tone of the paper he'd read, taking her through the part he'd witnessed. "Apparently, up to this point, your"—he corrected himself, avoiding the words *your father*—"they aren't satisfied. The monkeys still aren't psycho enough to suit them. Next they're going to add sharp brass spikes to the surrogate. The idea is, if one treatment doesn't work, try something worse."

Julie sat staring into space, a thoughtful frown marring her otherwise beautiful forehead. At length she said, "How do you know all this?"

He stared down into his drink. "What difference does it make?"

"It makes a lot of difference. Sometimes people make things up for their own reasons."

"It wasn't like that, Julie. I can't tell you where I got the information but—well, it's reliable."

"Secondhand information reliable?" she said in a scoffing tone. "Whoever told you this just doesn't know what he's talking about. In the first place, my father doesn't have a cruel bone in his body. He is the kindest, gentlest person

169

alive. And he loves animals. You should see him with Daisy. *You* make him sound like a monster."

"I didn't mean to. I'm sure your father's a great guy. So are a lot of scientists. It's just that he's doing one more experiment the world doesn't need."

Her gray eyes flashed. "Who are you to say that? How could you possibly know what he's trying for or how much the world might benefit from what he learns? I know my father. If he's doing what you say he is, then it's because he has a very good reason."

"The end justifies the means?"

She opened her mouth to respond, hesitated as if she'd had second thoughts, then apparently decided to plunge ahead. "You seemed to think the end justified the means when you used me to help publicize Laura's demonstration about the lamb."

"Hey, I apologized for that. I'd hoped we'd put it behind us."

She lowered her eyes. "There are other examples. What about raiding medical labs and destroying months or years of someone's work? You seem to think the end justifies the means there."

"That's different. People don't do that to hurt living creatures but to save them and call attention to atrocities no one would ever hear about otherwise."

"There are a lot of people who'd disagree with you."

Of course there were, but, until now, he'd thought she wasn't among them.

Before he could say so, she said, "That's not the point though. The point is I don't know where you got your information, but I *do* know my father. He's not cruel and he's

170

not stupid, and no one has a right to criticize him for something they know nothing about."

Jeff felt a nerve working in his jaw. "Well, I guess that takes care of that."

Her chin trembled slightly as she said, "I guess it does."

For a moment he wished he could somehow erase this whole conversation, that they could return to where they had been before the words were said. In the next breath, he decided that if that was the way she wanted things, it was all right with him. She had as good as called him a liar anyhow. There was no point in getting involved with someone who didn't believe in you or share your basic philosophy. What a jerk he'd been to think they had something special going.

"I think I'd better go home now," she said.

He picked up the check, reached into his pants pocket for change, and felt the duplicate of the lab key he'd had made earlier. His hand closed around it tightly. To think that he'd spent the whole day agonizing over whether he should turn it over to the ARS or not.

19

The following week Julie kept telling herself that her mother was right. The Ryders were a fanatical family, always worrying about a subject that most people never even concerned themselves with. If what she'd had with Jeff could be called a falling-out, that was all for the best. They would have had to part at the end of the school year anyhow. It was easier this way. Besides, she sometimes felt drained from being at odds with her mother so much. With Jeff out of her life, there was one less cause for friction.

At the same time she brooded about everything that had passed between them, going over in her mind what she had said to him, what he had said to her. How dare he use words like *cruel* and *stupid* about her father? She congratulated herself for her firm stand with him. A year ago she would never have had the strength to stand up to anybody. She was a different person now. Look at how she'd won out about the car, never bending to her mother's wishes, and every day this week driving back and forth to school on her own. Oh, yes, she was different all right—stronger.

Then why did she feel so empty inside, so low and almost weepy at times? Why did she keep remembering the afternoon of the picnic and the way Jeff had kissed her? And why were her dreams filled with pictures of even greater intimacies?

She still had lunch with Laura and her friends at school, but when Laura had asked her to her house one afternoon, Julie had begged off, saying she was just too swamped with homework.

"Are you sure that's the reason?" Laura asked. "Or does it have something to do with Jeff?"

Julie found she couldn't meet Laura's sharp blue eyes. "I really do have a lot of catching up to do."

Laura wouldn't accept that for an answer. "What happened with you two anyhow?"

Julie's spine stiffened. "I'd rather not talk about it."

Laura had thrown up her hands helplessly. "That's exactly what *he* says."

On that same afternoon Julie had received another college acceptance in the mail, this time from Stanford. All she could think of was how she and Jeff had both seemed to make Stanford a part of a dream world, too good to be true. How much easier life would have been, she thought, with fewer choices. She tucked the letter away in her desk next to the one from Yale. The longer she could delay, the longer she could hold on to the vision of independence the Stanford envelope offered.

She had no idea why she had so much difficulty in coming right out and asking her father exactly what his experiment was all about. Probably she would have had less trouble asking him about his love life. At any rate, she kept putting off questioning him, excusing herself with the thought that the act itself would prove she doubted him.

Her curiosity finally overcame her. One morning while her mother was still in bed, she caught him alone at breakfast. As she sipped her orange juice, she said, "You know, Dad, you never talk about your work. Why *is* that?"

Eyebrows raised, he gave her an exaggerated look of surprise. "Well! Whatever brought that on?"

"Oh, I don't know. I just got to thinking the other day that I don't know much about what you're working on, and I'd like to."

"I can't believe this," he said, an amused gleam in his eyes. "You've never shown any interest before."

"I know. And I've been trying to figure out why. I think it's because you and Mother never talk about it, so there's nothing to pique my interest."

"I don't talk about it with your mother because, beyond the fact that she's just not interested, the work isn't something that the layman can understand except in a general way."

"I don't know whether I can understand it or not, but I'm certainly interested. Right now, all I know is that you're doing some research in psychopathology. But I really don't know exactly what that means."

"Julie, that's a big subject for this early in the morning. I'd need a lot more time than I've got to explain. I'll tell you this much though: I'm studying something called separation neurosis. Now, do you know any more than you did in the first place?"

"I know what separation is and what neurosis is—but separation from what?" she persisted.

174

"In this case, the separation of infants from their mothers. We're learning about how the stress it causes leads to depression and neurosis."

Then Jeff must have had some of his facts straight. "Where did you ever find the infants to use?" she asked, deliberately feigning ignorance. Knowing her father, she believed that if she sounded critical, she would never get anything out of him.

He shot her a look, half surprised, half impatient. "I'm talking about animals—rhesus monkeys—not people."

"You mean, you separate newborn monkeys from their mothers?"

"How could we study them otherwise?"

"But couldn't you study human babies that are already separated from their mothers for one reason or another?"

"Do you suppose anyone is going to turn over human babies to us so that we can observe them in a controlled laboratory environment? You know better. We *have* to use animals."

"But to what purpose?"

He shook his head, his expression slightly amused. "I never thought I'd be defending myself to my own daughter, of all people. But so be it. Yes, there certainly is a purpose, although, I admit, a lot of research exists purely to add to a body of knowledge. The need to know for its own sake, I hope you realize, is a universal need. It doesn't always have to serve a purpose any greater than human curiosity.

"In this case, I'm planning to take a group of primates who've known nothing but the stress and depression of rejection and, in about a year's time, place them together. If they can learn to interact socially and raise normal offspring, it will indicate that psychological stress may not be irreparable—an important piece of information. My hope is that ultimately the study will advance our knowledge and help us deal with people who are similarly damaged."

Cruel? Stupid? Cruel to the monkeys, perhaps, but certainly not stupid, as Jeff had claimed. The experiment definitely had a worthy purpose. And yet, something still nagged at her. "Wouldn't it be better to work directly with troubled children? I mean, you'd have to do that eventually anyhow, wouldn't you?"

He studied her thoughtfully. "Does this have anything to do with that Ryder family? Your mother tells me they're big animal activists."

"I suppose it does have something to do with them. At least they've made me more conscious of how many millions of animals we sacrifice every year to our own needs."

The slight frown on his forehead told her he was growing annoyed now. "Let me tell you something, Julie," he said. "More than ninety percent of all new medical knowledge in the last century came from animal studies—immunization against polio, diphtheria, and measles, to name a few. And we're getting closer and closer to cures for cancer, diabetes, heart disease, and countless other illnesses because of those studies."

"But aren't there alternative methods?"

"There are some, of course—working with cell and tissue cultures and simulating the problem in a computer. But often, scientists don't know enough about how some biological systems work to create a model, so the use of live animals is absolutely essential. And, I must admit, I have no patience with people who, on the one hand, picket surgeons for learning their skills on animals and, on the other, expect those same surgeons to save the lives of their sick children."

176

"But what about the work *you're* doing? You can't call that medical."

She saw him stiffen. "A sick mind is just as important and just as 'medical' as a sick body. If you can justify the use of animals for one purpose, you can justify it for the other." Obviously through with the subject, he swallowed the last of his coffee and stood up, ready to leave.

Julie had to agree with him about the importance of sick minds. Still she persisted. "I'm sure I'd understand better if I could see what you're doing. Maybe I could visit the lab with you sometime."

"I'd love to take you, but I'm afraid that's impossible. Unauthorized people are just not admitted. There are too many important studies going on."

"I wouldn't interfere with anything."

"I know you wouldn't, but there are always ignorant people who can't keep their hands off things and could destroy months or years of work. That's why the rule—with no exceptions." He shrugged helplessly. "If it were up to me—"

He broke off and Julie said, "I understand."

He smiled at her, his expression fondly tolerant now. "As for my work, you're just going to have to trust your old dad's judgment. Okay?"

Julie nodded. He was very persuasive. He obviously believed it was necessary to sacrifice animals to human comfort and survival. All of which boiled down to the fact that some creatures must die so that others could live. She was more mixed up than ever.

As the days passed, in spite of her strong feelings of loyalty to her father, Julie began to soften and make excuses for Jeff. He simply didn't understand that there was another side to the picture. Besides, she missed him, missed the thought of him and the look of him, and the way he had made her begin to feel less of an outsider. He was far different from any prince of her dreams, yet that didn't seem to matter. If anything, the flesh-and-blood reality of him, with his stubbornness and his sometimes superior manner toward her, made him seem all the more attractive.

One evening, after listening to her mother extol the virtues of life in the East, Julie went to bed early to escape. At least she's no longer bugging me about more plastic surgery, Julie thought. The wound with its many tiny stitches was healing beautifully. As she settled in, Daisy hopped up beside her for her nightly cuddle. Julie held the little cat close and stroked her. "Poor Daisy," she said. "Nobody asked you if you wanted to be used for the benefit of others, did they? Nobody cared how much they hurt you." She kissed Daisy's scarred eye and sighed. "Nobody asked me either. At least, though, somebody came to *your* rescue."

20

" 'Vandals Raid University Lab,' " Laura read excitedly from a Santa Delores *Times* headline.

Jeff silently groaned. After he'd turned over the lab key to Cal Wallace, who had obviously passed it on to the Animal Liberation Army, Jeff had had second thoughts. He wished he'd never been involved. Yes, the lab needed a stringent clean-up. And, yes, that could be accomplished only if someone made the public aware of the deplorable conditions there. But why does the someone have to be me? he thought. Julie was no fool. Even if he apologized for talking about her father the way he had, she would never forgive him for his part in the raid if she knew. And he was sure she would guess.

"Let me see that," Jeff said, and took the paper from Laura. The article went on to tell how, on the night before last, over a hundred animals were spirited away, along with records, photographs, and video tapes. An anonymous member of the ALA had called the *Times* to claim responsibility, charging the university with housing animals in an unsanitary environment with shoddy, run-down, and negligent animal-care facilities. As he read on, he suddenly exclaimed, "Oh, no!"

"What's wrong?" Laura asked.

Relieved that his mother, still in bed, was not a part of the discussion, he read to Laura from the piece. " 'Dr. Harrison Peters, one of several university spokesmen, denied the charges. "The husbandry is good," he said. "The place is cleaned and the animals are watered and fed every day. The action of this group of irresponsible people is no better than Rambo-type vigilantism." ' "

"Uh-oh," Laura said. "I take it that's Julie's father."

"You know it."

The misery must have shown on his face, because Laura shot him a suspicious glance. "Why do I get the feeling that this has something to do with why you and Julie aren't speaking—or whatever it is you aren't doing?"

Jeff stared down into a bowl of cold cereal that looked highly unappetizing at the moment and said nothing.

"And all the time I thought your hormones had probably come on too strong for her." She paused, then suddenly a look of dawning came over her face. "Did you have something to do with the raid?"

He hesitated, then felt a great need to talk to someone about the situation. Two weeks had passed since his date with Julie and it was starting to feel like an eternity. He had grown more and more frustrated by their separation, like someone with important unfinished business that preyed on his mind and wouldn't let him rest. Just when he'd decided that he should make the first move to mend things between them, this had to happen. He said, "I gave the ARS a copy of the key to the lab, so I guess you could say I had something to do with the raid. They obviously turned it over to the Animal Liberation Army."

"Does Julie know?"

"She knew I was familiar with her father's work in the lab, but she didn't know about the key."

"Then don't tell her."

"That's easy enough," he said sarcastically. "She's not talking to me."

"And how did that happen, I'd like to know?"

Again Jeff hesitated. "Will you promise to keep it to yourself?"

"Of course. But what about Mom? Does she know?"

"No one knows—except you. The fewer people involved, the better. After all, what the ALA did is illegal. That makes me an accessory to a crime."

Laura gave a low whistle. "I never thought of it that way, but you're right. Don't worry. I won't say anything. I can be a real clam when I want to."

That was true. You could always trust Laura when something important was at stake. He gave her a detailed account of his visit to the lab. When he finished, looking appalled, she said, "Wow! I'm sure glad they raided the place. I only wish I'd been part of it."

"I'd be glad too, if it weren't for Julie." He went on to tell her about his date with Julie and how he had unthinkingly blurted out what he thought of her father's experiment. "I didn't mean to hurt her. I wish now I'd kept my big mouth shut."

Laura regarded him thoughtfully. "So that's what's bothering her."

"Well, you can't blame her. If it was anyone but her father, I know she would have agreed with me, but I have a strong feeling that she can't bear to think of her dad as anything less than a hero. So what do I do now?"

"You're asking *me* for advice? I'm not 'Dear Abby,' " Laura said, and in the next breath proceeded to advise him. "I'll tell you this, though. If you want to get back with Julie, you'll never do it if you don't start talking to her."

"What if *she* won't talk to me?"

"Well, you won't know that if you don't try her out, will you? Besides, if you start by apologizing for the things you said about her father, she'll have to listen. I mean, it's only civilized. At least that should get you started."

"What about my part in the raid?"

"That's easy. You can't tell anyone about that anyhow. There are too many other people involved."

"She'll guess though. I'm sure she will."

"Listen, if she really likes you and doesn't want to believe it, she won't."

"But then I'd be a phony. What I did is me. If she can't accept that, then she can't accept me."

Laura rolled her eyes. "Look, you asked me, and I told you. If you want to play Saint Jefferson and do things the hard way, then don't ask 'Dear Abby.' Consult your nearest clergyman. If you want to do things the easy way—lie!"

Oh, sure. It was easy enough for someone like Laura who wasn't emotionally involved to treat the whole thing lightly. Not so for Jeff. He thought of Julie with her green-flecked gray eyes that always looked at him without a trace of guile. How could you lie to someone like that?

On the same morning at breakfast, Julie's father, his face livid, sounded off to her mother. "They're nothing but a bunch of hooligans. I suppose they thought it was some kind of lark, destroying months, even years, of important work. My God, Anne, they took every one of my monkeys. Every one!" He shook his head somberly. "I think you were right. It was a mistake to come out here. A big mistake."

Anne Peters nodded sympathetically. "What are you going to do about it?"

"I just don't know. It's too late in the semester to start again." He sighed hopelessly. "Honestly, I am so sickened by this whole affair that I don't even feel like going in this morning."

"But you will," his wife said. "If you ask me, this would never have happened in a more prestigious university. They'd have had better security."

Julie listened as they talked, aware that her mother was delighted with the turn of events and that her father was now only too willing to let her lead the way. Julie couldn't blame him. His work, the one reason he'd been willing to come out here, was destroyed.

The raid had come as a shock to her. And yet, as she thought about it now, it somehow seemed inevitable, the natural progression of events going from bad to worse, and all centering around her father's work. First, the words with Jeff. Now, this.

The thought ran through her head that if Jeff was familiar with her father's experiment, he must also have had a more extensive knowledge of the lab. Could he have somehow been involved?

Almost as if he had read her mind, her father glanced at her sharply. "That Ryder boy you went out with—doesn't his whole family belong to the group responsible for this raid?"

"Oh, no, Dad," Julie said quickly. "They belong to the

Animal Rights Society. That's a different organization entirely. They don't raid labs or do anything like that." She didn't mention that they were in complete sympathy with the ALA and even helped them find homes for rescued animals. She had no wish to see Jeff in trouble any more than she had her father. Besides, no matter what she suspected, she had no proof.

"You're quite sure?" her father said.

"Oh, yes."

"Well, I wouldn't want to point a finger at innocent people, but believe me, I'd like to see this whole terrorist gang in jail where they belong."

Her mother, clad in a simple but elegant white caftan, rose from the table, saying she was going to shower. Before she left the room she turned to Julie. "I'm not saying that boy had anything to do with this raid, but it wouldn't surprise me if he had. It's all too typical of people who join fanatical groups. In the future, I hope you'll choose your friends more carefully."

The words made Julie bristle. "You make them sound like creeps, Mother. They're not. I *know* them, and they're good people."

"Then Lord save us from all good people," her mother said. "Believe me, I just can't wait for this semester to end. We can't get back to civilization soon enough to suit me."

Julie swallowed the words that came to her mouth. After her mother left the room, she said to her father, "Why does Mother always have to be so down on this place?"

"After what happened the other night, I'm beginning to feel that way myself. The raid set me back to Square One. I don't know what I'll do now. But I *do* know this, your mother will never be happy until we're all back East."

184

How well Julie knew.

For the next few days articles appeared in the paper, several critical of the work and conditions in the lab. The nightly television news presented an interview with a masked member of the ALA who defended the raid and gave a brief picture of some of the experiments they had interrupted, among them Julie's father's. Although he mentioned no names, he made the baby monkey study sound like an exercise in sadism, then assured the public that all the infants were now in good hands, those of *real,* not cloth, surrogate mothers.

Julie had never before seen her easygoing, normally preoccupied father so angry. He'd stab his finger at each critical article in the paper and say things like "Look at that, they don't know what they're talking about. Don't they understand this is all done for their benefit?" or "Who are they to criticize people who have worked in their fields for years and made all kinds of advances for humanity?"

Finally, Julie said, "If you have to start all over anyhow, couldn't you try something new—maybe a study with people?"

"Oh, God," he exclaimed. "Now they've convinced even you that I'm some kind of monster."

"I didn't mean that, Dad. I just figured that there were lots of unknowns about people."

"Julie, this happens to be my area of interest. I do it because I believe what we will learn from it will help humans. And, yes, I just happen to think that's important. I also believe that the welfare of humans comes before the welfare of animals, although, sometimes, what helps one helps the other."

"But Dad—"

"Julie, I know how some people feel about all this, and I

185

understand that you may share those feelings. Remember, I do love you, and I care about how you think of me. Yet, in spite of all that, I have to do what I believe right. And I believe, with all my heart, that my work is right, is important, and is proper."

Julie nodded soberly. She couldn't honestly say he was wrong.

21

Jeff stood outside Kennedy High, trying to spot Julie amid the swarms of exiting students. He saw Laura, arm in arm with Brian, oblivious to anyone but each other as they joined the stream heading for the parking lot. He also saw Laura's special group of girl friends but no Julie.

As the crowd thinned to a few stragglers, he was about to give up when he spied her, all alone, book bag over her shoulder, looking, at a glance, not very different from any other high school girl, a look, he suspected, she tried to cultivate. He also suspected she was unaware that no matter how she attempted to downplay her appearance, the way she carried her tall, slender body would always turn heads. You would never guess that, underneath it all, she had the same human frailties and insecurities as the rest of us. In fact, he thought, her regal posture could have been a defense against showing how vulnerable she really was.

He approached her, not at all sure she would even speak to him. "Hi," he said.

Obviously taken by surprise, her face started to light up—

at least he could have sworn it did—with a radiance that quickly dimmed and was replaced with a guarded look.

"Can we go someplace where we can talk?" he asked.

"What about?"

"About us." She seemed to hesitate, so he added, "If you don't want to go anyplace, at least let me walk you to your car. You *are* driving these days, aren't you?"

"Yes, I'm driving—thanks to you."

"Hey, I wasn't fishing for a show of gratitude or anything like that." He gave her a mischievous smile. "Not that I don't deserve it." When she didn't respond to his humor, he mentally kicked himself and fell into step beside her as she headed toward the parking lot.

For a moment he was at a loss as to how to begin. Then he simply plunged in. "Julie, I know I hurt your feelings and I'm sorry—I'm really sorry. I should have realized how you feel about your dad and not criticized him the way I did."

She shrugged. "You said what you thought."

"But I didn't have to say anything. I could have kept it to myself."

"But you would have thought it, and that's pretty much the same thing, isn't it?"

"Not really. I mean, no matter how I might feel about someone's parents, it wouldn't have anything to do with how I felt about the someone." He'd wanted to sound cool. Instead, he realized, he sounded awkward.

To his relief, they had reached her car now, and she gave her attention to unlocking the door and extricating herself from her book bag, which she threw on the floor. Then she turned to Jeff and this time smiled at him. "I understand how you feel about my father's work, and no, I don't hold it against you. You have every right to your opinion. And no, it's not a case of like me, like my father."

"Whew! I don't mind telling you that's a big relief. Not that I dislike your father or anything like that—I hardly know him. I just hoped maybe, as they say, you could see your way clear to forgiving and forgetting." Again he was afraid he wasn't sounding as cool as he'd meant to.

Instead of responding directly to his words, she said, "Maybe my father's experiment wasn't anything *you* would approve of, but it *was* important to him."

"Of course," Jeff said, but he was merely mouthing words. He couldn't come anyplace close to feeling sorry for Harrison Peters. In fact, he'd been hoping that by some wild stretch of the imagination the raid wouldn't even come up in his and Julie's conversation.

Julie said, "He's so upset about everything that he's decided to look for a position back East."

Jeff's stomach tightened. "Does that mean you'll be going to Yale?"

"I suppose so. If Dad had stayed at Santa Delores, it would have made sense to go to a school in California, but, as it is—" She shrugged helplessly.

Jeff felt as if someone had just kicked him in the gut. Julie was going back East, and he was responsible. That little act of handing a key to Cal Wallace had come full circle to whisk Julie right out of his life. He thought now that she looked as miserable as he felt. "You don't have to go to an eastern college just because your folks move back there."

"No, but it seems like the reasonable thing to do."

All Jeff could think of was the talk they'd had the day of the picnic. You didn't have to be a psychologist to realize

189

that what she'd wanted then was to get free of her mother's domination. "I really thought you were going for your independence."

"I guess it just wasn't meant to be. If it hadn't been for this raid—well, things might have been different."

Without thinking, Jeff said, "Please don't let the raid keep you from doing what you want to do. I'd never forgive myself if that—" He broke off, suddenly conscious that he was giving himself away.

She stared at him, her eyes widening. "You *were* a part of it."

For a long moment, he stared back in silence. Lie, Laura had said. He swallowed hard. "I wasn't in on the raid, Julie. Honest."

He saw a look of relief wash over her face. "Then you didn't have anything to do with it."

He opened his mouth to follow Laura's advice, then just couldn't do it. "I said I wasn't in on the raid. I didn't say I didn't have anything to do with it. I don't want to lie to you, Julie. I'm afraid I'm sort of responsible for the whole thing."

"Oh," she said in a flat voice. "I don't suppose you'd care to tell me how."

"I'd rather not."

She shook her head, a look of anguish on her face. "You don't know what you've done to my father—to a lot of people—even to me."

He almost wished now that he'd lied. "If I've hurt you— or anyone else—that wasn't my intention, and I'm sorry. But I just can't be sorry that the lab was cleaned out. And I don't think it was wrong—any more than I would have thought it wrong for someone to have rescued people from

190

the gas ovens of concentration camps. I'd be a liar if I said anything different."

She was silent for a long moment. Finally, she said, "How do you know I won't tell my father?"

"I don't. But I have to take that chance. If you think it will help anything to tell him—well, go ahead. I'll understand."

She said nothing, but he was only too well aware of the pain in her eyes as she turned away and stepped into her car. He stood watching as she started the engine and even as she drove off. How ironical, he thought, that in doing what he believed right, he had lost the respect of the person he wanted most to impress.

Much later that afternoon Jeff arrived home to find his mother alone in the house and starting dinner.

"Where's Laura?" he asked.

"Out with Brian—where else? Honestly, Jeff, I don't know how to get through to that girl. I came home early and surprised her here with him. She knows how I feel about that. You *did* tell her that time you talked to her, didn't you?"

"Yes, I told her."

"Well, it didn't take then. Of course she said they had only stopped here to pick up a paper she was working on, and then they were heading for the library. I don't know whether to believe her or not. I think you'd better talk to her again."

He couldn't help frowning. He had spent the time since he'd left Julie driving around aimlessly, thinking. Now he was so immersed in his own problems that he wasn't in the mood to take on anyone else's. "Laura isn't going to pay any attention to me, Mom. We just don't have that kind of relationship. I can't tell her what to do. She has a mind of her own."

"You're wrong, Jeff. She pays more attention to you than she ever would to me. Besides, I depend on your help that way."

She might as well have said, *You're the man of the family now.* In his present frame of mind, the words sat uncomfortably on his shoulders. He merely grunted.

She seemed to take that as assent and changed the subject. "I ran into Cal Wallace today in that little place near the office where I eat. He treated me to lunch. Wasn't that nice of him?"

"Great."

"Why didn't you tell me about the part you played in the lab raid?"

"He told you that!"

"Well, of course, he didn't tell me exactly what you did, but he intimated that they have you to thank."

"But he wasn't supposed to say anything."

"Oh, Jeff," she said in a chiding voice. "Cal knows he can trust me—as much work as I've done for the ARS! You should know you can trust me, too."

"Mom, they told me the fewer people who knew, the better."

"Well, never mind, I forgive you." She gave him an all-embracing smile. "Your dad would have been so proud of you."

Somehow that didn't make Jeff feel any better. He nodded and moved to leave the kitchen.

"Just a minute," she said, and scooped up and handed

him some pamphlets that, until now, he hadn't noticed on the kitchen table. "I stopped at the travel agency near the office to see what I could pick up on San Diego."

"San Diego?" he said, bewildered.

"For that trip we're going to take this summer. You remember."

Oh, yes. The trip that Laura had so smoothly wriggled out of.

His mother went on and on about what a fun spot San Diego would be. There was the ocean and countless points of interest, and it would be only a hop, a skip, and a jump to Mexico for a day's excursion.

"Great," Jeff said, although he had never meant anything less. He took the brochures, went on to his room, and tossed them on his desk without a glance. His mind, as it had done all day, went back to Julie. Would she tell her father and make it impossible for Jeff to remain at the university? What she couldn't know, of course, was that staying in Santa Delores while she went to a school thousands of miles away was punishment enough. What was even worse was the thought that she would always hate even the memory of him. On the other hand, he could see himself measuring every new girl he met by her.

Why? They'd never even come close to doing anything you could call making out. And yet, after their shared confidences, he'd begun to feel closer to her than to any girl he'd ever known. He recalled how, on the day of their picnic, he'd said to her, "You realize, don't you, that you may have straightened out my whole life." And, at that moment, everything had seemed so clear.

He picked up the pamphlets his mother had given him. As he stared at them without interest, she poked her head in the door and, holding what looked like a couple of tickets, exclaimed, "Look what I've got."

He glanced up at her questioningly.

"They're tickets to next Thursday's concert. One of the agents in the office has a season pass. He's busy that night so, *voilà.*" She waved the tickets in the air. "I thought we'd let Laura get her own dinner that night. We'll eat out and go on from there."

All the frustration and resentment that Jeff had so long buried surfaced. "I can't go to a concert next Thursday night. I have an important exam on Friday."

"But I'm giving you plenty of notice."

"It doesn't matter. I'll need Thursday night to cram." That wasn't exactly the truth, but it was close enough. Exam or not, he needed every minute he could find to study. Besides, the last thing on earth he felt like doing was attending a concert, especially with his mother. "Maybe Laura will go with you."

"Oh, Laura—she has no time for anyone but Brian." She sighed and glanced down at the tickets. "I really thought it would be a big treat. Well, I may as well give them to someone else. I'm certainly not going by myself."

"Can't you ask someone else?"

"I don't know who. Besides, I don't think it's too much to expect the members of my own family to spend an occasional night out with me."

At any other time Jeff would have relented and gone. Today her demands weighed too heavily upon him. "I can't go to the concert on Thursday," he said, a quiver in his voice. Then he found himself blurting, "And I can't go to San Diego either—or anyplace else this summer. I'm working in Uncle Dan's law office, the way I did last year."

194

She stared at him, displeasure showing plainly on her face. "You never told me."

"I just made up my mind." That was the truth. Not that he hadn't been thinking about it all along, but now he was suddenly aware of how empty Santa Delores would seem without Julie. He had to get away, not only from the town but from his mother's constant need for a companion. "I just made up my mind about something else, too. I'm not going back to Santa Delores next year." He stuck his chin out as if defying anyone to challenge him. "I'm going to Stanford."

"You're what?" she exclaimed.

"I applied to Stanford and they accepted me. I didn't tell you because I didn't think anything would come of it."

She shook her head confusedly. "I don't understand what's going on here. Don't you realize that I can't afford a school like that? I mean, there will be living expenses as well as tuition."

"I have it all worked out. I talked to Uncle Dan about it. He's sure he can help me get a scholarship, and I can work part-time in his law office."

"I see," she said coldly. "You and that brother of mine have both worked out everything behind my back. All my plans don't mean a thing."

"It's not like that. I—well, sure, I've always been interested in going to a school like Stanford, but I never seriously thought of applying until Uncle Dan mentioned the scholarship. Even then, I didn't think I'd do anything about it. Now, I realize I have to. I hoped you'd understand, because it really means a lot to me."

"What about what your father wanted? He expected you to go to Santa Delores—maybe even teach there someday."

195

"I know. And he expected me to become a wildlife biologist. Well, I'm just not sure that's what I want to do. And I can't do it just because it was what Dad wanted. I've got to find my own way."

"I don't know what to say—you and Laura both going off at the same time." Her eyes clouded. "First, I lose your father, now both of you. I feel as though I'm losing everyone I love."

"You're not losing us. We'll both be home often. Neither one of us will be that far." Stanford was about a hundred miles distant, but Jeff could drive that easily in a couple of hours. Laura would be even closer at the school of her choice, Colton College, which was only fifty miles away.

"I don't know what I'll do—all by myself."

She looked so lost he almost felt sorry for her, then he reminded himself that this was the pose she always struck to gain his sympathy. He made up his mind that nothing she could say or do would change anything now. For the first time since he'd toyed with the idea of going to Stanford, he felt totally committed and it felt great. "We'll come home a lot on weekends or you can come to see us."

She shook her head. "You may as well know that I don't approve of this at all. With all the unnecessary expense and everything else, it sounds like a very foolish move. But if you're so determined, I suppose there's nothing I can do to stop you." She waited expectantly for a response. When he said nothing, she turned on her heel, her expression hurt and angry, and marched out of the room.

For a moment, Jeff's resolve faltered. But only for a moment. He retrieved the Stanford letter of acceptance from his desk and immediately set about answering it. Before he could change his mind, he went out and posted it in the corner mailbox. There, the deed was done!

Still, all night long, he couldn't help accusing himself of being some kind of monster. And all the following week he wondered if he should relent and, at least, offer to go with her to the concert. To his surprise, when Thursday night rolled around, Cal Wallace came to pick her up. And she had never even said a word about asking him.

Well, I guess life goes on, Jeff thought. That had just never occurred to him before.

22

Ever since her date with Jeff, Julie had gone through the motions of living with a dull ache inside her. Her mother's jubilation at anticipating a move back East made her feel even more depressed. She asked herself what she had to look forward to once she was back in the old life. Another breakdown?

Along with everything else, she was troubled about her father. He not only was the sweet, gentle man she had always adored and looked up to, now she had to recognize that he had a darker side, that of the cold, insensitive scientist. Yet, in spite of how she or anyone else regarded his experiments, she had to feel sorry for him. He seemed bewildered by the condemnation he and other university scientists were receiving in the press and deeply disturbed. His only defense was a hostile and superior attitude toward all his critics, protesting that they were simply incapable of understanding.

As for telling her father that Jeff had somehow made the raid possible, that was an option she had rejected as quickly as the thought had occurred to her. Enough people were already hurt. Besides, although a part of her remained loyal to her father, another part sympathized with Jeff and his goals.

It seemed strange now to think of what high hopes she had had when she and her parents had first come to Santa Delores. She'd looked forward to a new and fulfilling life. Now the only thing she could picture was all three of them slinking away, complete failures.

She'd had one real success though—getting her driver's license. She loved every moment she spent in her little car, driving back and forth to school and dreaming up any excuse to take her out on the road.

One afternoon after school, telling herself that her car could use a good run, she headed out on the highway that led to the desert. Remembering how she and Jeff had taken the same route to visit Mercedes Damsen made Julie more conscious than ever of how mixed up and unhappy she felt about Jeff and her father and everything else. Mercedes had seemed to possess an almost spiritual satisfaction with her life that Julie recalled with envy. She had a strong urge to see the woman again.

Julie stopped at a gas station and used the pay phone to call Mercedes to ask if she remembered her and if it would be all right to pay a short visit.

"Julie Peters—you're the pretty girl who came out with Jeff Ryder a while back. Of course I remember you. And, by all means, come on out. I'd love to see you again."

Thirty minutes later Julie found herself seated across from Mercedes in the ranch house living room and drinking an herbal tea that tasted faintly of raspberries. The thought occurred to her that some of the animals from the lab, including her father's monkeys, might well be secreted away on the property. If so, she really didn't want to know. She was certainly not there as a spy.

"I see you got your license since you were here last," Mercedes said. Essex, her golden retriever, lay close at her feet.

"Yes, but I haven't had it very long. That's why I thought it would do me good to get used to driving farther than just back and forth to school."

"Very wise. The more practice you get, the easier you'll feel on the road." Mercedes's aquamarine-blue eyes studied Julie curiously. "No Jeff today?"

Julie lowered her eyes. "Oh . . . no."

To her surprise, Mercedes said, "Lovers' spat?"

Julie reddened. "Oh, no. There isn't anything like that between us," she said too quickly.

Mercedes's eyes glinted with amusement. "Friends' spat then?"

What made the woman so perceptive? Julie opened her mouth to say that she hadn't quarreled with Jeff, then suddenly realized that she was hurting to tell someone, and that very hurt had unconsciously directed her here. "We didn't quarrel, exactly. I guess you could say we had a difference of opinion."

"Serious?"

"I'm afraid so."

"Want to tell me about it?"

"There's not much to tell," Julie said, then found herself talking about the raid and the effect it had had upon her father. "Jeff admits he was responsible," she said when she'd finished, knowing that Mercedes, sympathetic to his cause, would never turn him in. "I guess I just don't know whose side I'm on."

"I see," Mercedes said. "I didn't realize your father was involved." She contemplated her jeans-clad legs stretched out in front of her. "Now you're torn between the two men in your life."

A self-conscious smile flickered across Julie's face. "In a way. But it's more than that. Everything seems to boil down to vivisection and where I stand on the issue. Sometimes I feel as passionately against it as Jeff and his sister Laura. Other times I just don't know."

"Especially when your father's involved?"

"There's that, yes." Julie stared down into her teacup. "I wondered how you felt about it."

Mercedes laughed. "You mean you'd trust asking an animal nut like me?"

Julie shrugged. "Somehow I felt you must have thought it through objectively at some time."

"Julie, I'll be glad to give you my thinking on the subject, but I can't make any claim to objectivity. I've always cared about the helpless. That goes for people as well as animals. I've thought a lot about it and read a lot about it. I know which side I'm on and why. That's all I can tell you."

"I guess that's all I want to hear. For instance, Jeff and Laura claim that we use millions of animals every year to experiment on in any way we see fit. They think there shouldn't be *any* animal use at all."

"Julie, in a perfect world we wouldn't use animals for any kind of experiments—medical or otherwise—any more than we now use humans."

"And you're going to say that the world's not perfect."

"Yes. The world's not perfect. But if we're here for anything—and everyone's always wondering why we were put on this earth—it's to use the wherewithal God gave us to go

201

on from where he left off and make the world as close to perfect as we can."

"But my father would say that that's why we have all this research—to make a better world—even if we have to use animals."

"That's just it. I'm not sure we'll have a better world. A society that is indifferent to the suffering of animals is also indifferent to the suffering of people. The two go hand in hand. How many of us already abuse humans physically—and just as important, mentally? Too often we're willing to sacrifice our own children to our needs, for example. And there are others.

"But right this minute, I want to be realistic. I know, and all the animal rights groups know, that the use of animals is not going to disappear for a long, long time. If nothing else, there are too many people who benefit personally from grants of money that allow them to carry on their work."

Julie thought of her father. "But what if the work is something that helps humans and, as my father says, adds to our store of knowledge?"

"I can only answer that by quoting George Bernard Shaw. 'You do not settle whether an experiment is justified or not be merely showing that it is of some use. The distinction is not between useful and useless experiments, but between barbarous and civilized behavior. Vivisection is a social evil because if it advances human knowledge, it does so at the expense of human character.' "

"If you believe that, then no animals would be used," Julie said.

"That's right. And the only reason we can use them at all is because they have no voice in the matter."

True, Julie thought, but at least they had people like Jeff and Laura to speak for them.

"But, as I said, giving up the use of animals entirely isn't realistic. In our time, those of us who consider it a moral issue probably can't hope to accomplish as much as we'd like, I'm sorry to say." Essex, her dog, made a guttural sound as a bid for attention. She took a minute to rub his head. When he gazed up at her with adoring eyes, she said, "You know we're talking about you, don't you, boy?"

After a moment she picked up her thread of thought. "No, I'm afraid all we can really do is to try to raise people's consciousness until they stop using animals for purposes that only satisfy human vanity and for experiments that are unnecessary."

Again, thinking of her father, Julie said, "What would you call unnecessary?"

"Oh—things like trying to drive animals crazy by strapping them down and burning them, freezing them, drowning them, starving them, battering their skulls, force-feeding them with caustic substances, depriving them of food and water until they submit to twelve-hundred-volt shocks of electricity— all these horrors and more."

Julie said, indignantly, "I find it very hard to believe that anyone has ever done anything like that."

"Of course you do. But it's all been documented—and usually by the people who have performed the experiments."

"But they must have had a good reason," Julie persisted.

"That's what I question. That's where we need someone to strictly monitor this business, to stop the many redundant experiments and to judge whether the end is worth the means. All most of us ask is that we at least make a start."

Julie thought of some of Laura's big objections. "You mean like not sacrificing animals for fur coats or using them for cosmetic research—things we can live easily without. And not taking people's former pets from the pound and turning them over to someone for vivisection." She could go along with all that.

"Yes, that and more. We can also start taking responsibility for the choices we make every day to keep ourselves healthy and to produce healthy children. Then we won't need miracle cures for diseases that could have been prevented in the first place. More lives have been saved by sanitation, you know, than by antibiotics."

"What about for food?" Julie asked.

"I'm not even going to get into that one. I don't eat animals myself, but I'm well aware that most people do, and it isn't easy to change the eating habits of a lifetime. Nevertheless, I think the problem will ultimately take care of itself as people come to understand that eating meat shortens their lives."

Julie said thoughtfully, "My mother has just cut out all red meat because my father finally convinced her it's bad for the heart. We only have chicken and fish in our house now."

"That's the start I'm talking about." Mercedes smiled wistfully. "There, you see, I told you I was biased."

Indeed she was, Julie thought on the way home. But she was also a very together lady, idealistic, yet with her feet on the ground. Fight the smaller battles, the ones you have a chance of winning, she seemed to be saying, and perhaps, someday, you just might win the war.

Mercedes's words were still ringing in Julie's ears the following afternoon while she sat at the desk in her bedroom, staring down at the pages of her American history book, yet seeing none of the words. Daisy lay curled on the bed, sleeping.

Julie's mother interrupted the quiet scene when she came into the room and said, "Have you answered the Yale letter yet?"

"Not yet."

"Well, get with it. Time's running out."

"I will, Mother." Julie had yet to respond to any of the colleges that had accepted her, even Yale. She asked herself what she was waiting for. She had already settled the matter in her mind. She was going to Yale.

Her mother sat down on the bed to fondle Daisy. "I know you've got a lot on your mind this year. I'll be so glad when the term ends for both you and your father. The minute you graduate, you and I are heading back to New York. Your father can follow as soon as he finishes up at the university. He doesn't know what he's going to do yet, but in any case, we're going to put the house up for sale."

Julie's stomach tightened. "When?"

"Next week."

So soon, Julie thought.

"They tell me it will probably take quite a while to find a buyer."

"Is that what Mrs. Ryder said?"

"Mrs. Ryder?" Her mother acted as if she'd never heard the name. "Oh, her . . . No, I'm putting the place in the hands of another realtor who, I think, can do better for us."

Knowing how her mother felt about the Ryders, Julie wasn't surprised. If anything, she was relieved, she told herself. The less she saw of Jeff's family, the less she was reminded of him and that was all to the good. She had even arranged to avoid his sister at school by driving home to

lunch and dashing off to accomplish fabricated errands whenever an intimate moment with Laura threatened. Which was
not so often these days. Julie kept to herself, and the rest
of the students, used to her presence now, left her to herself.
And that was all right too. So why did she feel so lonely, so
bereft?

"I talked to Morgan this morning," her mother said as
she absently scratched Daisy's head. "After the Scottish stint,
she may line up something else for you in Europe this summer."

"Oh?" Julie's stomach lurched.

"Morgan was absolutely ecstatic when I told her you'd be
going to Yale. With you so close to New York, she'll be able
to find you enough work in your free time to at least keep
your face before the public. You know how important that
is."

Yes, she knew how important that was. She had thought
that after months of absence Morgan would have considered
her no longer a salable commodity. That was obviously not
the case. She was suddenly aware that her head was starting
to ache.

Her mother rose and beamed at Julie. "Don't look so
glum. We're both going to have a lovely time this summer.
Your father can join us in Europe if he wants to and we'll
all get in some sightseeing."

Julie gave a weak smile.

"Now I'm going to get myself a cup of tea. Do you want
anything?"

"No."

"All right then. I'll leave you to your work. Don't forget
to write that letter to Yale."

Julie nodded. As soon as she was alone in her room, she

became aware that her head was pounding now and her stomach churning. She could feel herself standing in front of the camera again, smiling joyously, innocently, coquettishly, sensually, smiling like a robot with the same old phony adjectives raining over her head—*terrific! beautiful! fantastic! super!* All the progress she'd made with Dr. Almquist was quickly vanishing before the vision of that other Julie.

"*. . . You look the part, so everyone expects it of you, and that's what you do. What about you? Is it what you want to do?*" Jeff's words, spoken that day after the visit to Mercedes, came back to her. What *about* me? she asked herself. *Is there any me?*"

She got up and stretched out on the bed beside Daisy, gently stroking the cat. Daisy yawned. "I'm not very different from you," Julie said softly. "You and my father's monkeys and all the other animals people use any way they see fit."

What was it Mercedes had said? "*The only reason we can use them at all is because they have no voice in the matter.*"

No voice in the matter.

"Maybe I am different from you," she murmured.

Julie went back to her desk to spend the next half hour answering all the university letters she had let wait so long. Then she hurried out and drove to the nearest post office to slip the envelopes into the appropriate slot. There, that took care of that! Not quite, she reminded herself. There was still her mother to face.

She headed home, where she found Anne Peters in the living room, curled up on the divan with a copy of *The New Yorker*. Julie sat stiffly on a seat facing her and, when her mother looked up, took a deep breath and said simply, "I don't want to upset you. But I just can't do it."

Her mother looked half amused, half curious. "Can't do what?"

The words rushed out. "I can't take any more modeling jobs, and I can't go to Yale. I'm going to Stanford."

"You're what?"

"I'm going to Stanford."

Anne Peters straightened in her seat and leaned forward. "Do you mind telling me what this is all about?"

"I'll try, Mother." Julie took a moment to pull herself together, then continued. "I don't want to go back East because I don't want to go back to modeling—at least, not now. And maybe never."

"Julie, I had no intention of working you too hard, if that's what you think. I shouldn't have to remind you that if you're out of the public eye too long they won't want you back."

"It doesn't matter. For once in my life I want to know how it feels to live like other people. And I've found out that it's going to take time to learn. I have to practice making my own decisions and standing by myself and doing all the things I need to do to grow up." She gave a deep sigh. "I just can't go back to the world I came from. I feel suffocated every time I think of it."

"Are you trying to tell me that I don't have your welfare at heart? That I suffocate you?" her mother said indignantly.

"Oh, not intentionally. And maybe with somebody else, it wouldn't work that way. I just wish I could be the person you want me to be, but I can't. I've tried, but I always feel as though I'm being squeezed into a box that I can't get out of, and the longer I'm in it, the more oxygen I use up until I can't breathe at all."

Her mother slapped the magazine closed. "Julie, if you're trying to place some kind of guilt trip on me, you're succeeding. You think that I caused your breakdown, don't you?"

"I'm not trying to place blame, Mother. All I know is that there's a time for everything and this is my time to be on my own. I have to find out if I'm a real person. Up to now, the only me I know is someone in a photograph. I feel as though I need time to store things inside me—humor, knowledge, love—things like that—before I can ever come to life."

"But I fail to see why you can't do that at Yale as well as at Stanford. No one's going to force you to model if you really don't want to."

Julie gave a wry smile. "Mother, whether you mean to be or not, you're always very persuasive. I need to be out of temptation's way."

"Out of my way, you mean." Anne Peters shook her head sadly. "I'm having a hard time taking this all in. I had no idea you felt so bitter toward me."

"I don't feel bitter," Julie protested.

Her mother didn't seem to hear the words. "This has been my life, too. I thought I was building something wonderful and now I learn that it was all for nothing—all wasted."

This is even harder than facing a camera, Julie thought. But I'm doing it. *I'm actually doing it!* And the world isn't ending. "But your work hasn't been wasted, for either of us. We've both learned a lot. You've been a wonderful manager and, with all you know, you could start your own agency if you wanted to. You could handle other girls."

Her mother dismissed the idea with a toss of her head. "I've never given anything like that a thought."

"But maybe you should."

"Start my own agency? Morgan would simply love that."

"You could do it, Mother."

209

"I don't think so," she said, shaking her head, all the while staring into space. "You'd have to start small with only a few clients." Then she shook her head again. "No. Out of the question."

At least I've planted the seed, Julie thought. She knew very well her mother wasn't happy with her decision, and it was going to take a while before she could accept it, but accept it she would and eventually she would learn to live with it.

I'm not a child anymore, Julie thought, and I do have a voice. I just have to learn how to use it.

23

A warm June sun flooded the Kennedy High patio where gowned students and their parents gathered after the baccalaureate address. PTA members had set up a long table decorated festively with flowers and offering an assortment of goodies to go with afternoon tea. Graduation was still to come, and Julie, uncomfortably hot, wished the gowns could have been reserved for that occasion alone. She could see Laura and her mother near the table but no Jeff. Had he deliberately avoided the ceremony because of her?

The speaker, a former astronaut, had talked about attainment, calling his speech "Reaching for the Stars." The only part that remained with Julie was his assessment of the space shuttle catastrophe when he'd said, "We must never sacrifice integrity to reach our goals, no matter how desirable or worthy those goals seem."

The statement only served to remind Julie of the talk she'd had with Mercedes and which, when all was said and done, always came back to the same question: Does the end justify the means? Apparently the speaker didn't think so. And yet, on the other side, social activists always pointed out that with their goals, change came only after civil disobedience. Too often, Julie had to agree with them.

Her father was deep in conversation with one of the teachers who had spotted him and come charging over to introduce himself with "You probably don't remember me, but—" It seemed he had taken her father's class at Columbia about five years ago. Now they were deep into a long conversation about their days at Columbia.

Julie's mother had begged off attending the ceremony, pleading back strain brought on, she maintained, by the stress of another move. Julie suspected the stress was really related to the stand Julie had taken which would ultimately separate her from her mother. Not only would Julie have to learn to operate independently, but so would Anne.

As her father talked, Julie had time to glance around at the laughing, chatting groups, feeling a deep loneliness, aware of how much she'd hoped for this year and how, with Jeff, she'd let the promise of a close relationship slip through her fingers.

Now it was too late to do anything about it. And even if it were not, she would still have no idea how to go about mending the rift between them. After all, she wasn't exactly such a scintillating personality that anyone was itching to be a part of her life. Jeff certainly wouldn't have to look hard to find someone more interesting. She sighed sadly to think that today was no different from every other landmark occasion of her life. She always took inventory and always came up wanting.

"Hi," a voice said at her elbow. She turned to find Laura beside her. "Wow, these things are hot." Laura pulled out the neck of her gown and blew down inside it. Then she

212

grabbed Julie's hand. "Come on, the lunch gang wants to see you."

Julie felt a warm rush of pleasure to think that someone—anyone—wanted to see her. "I'll be right back, Dad," she told her father. He nodded and went on talking.

Laura pulled her through and away from the crowd and, to Julie's surprise, headed around the corner of one of the buildings. "Where are you going?" she started to say and, in the next breath, understood. Jeff stood there, obviously waiting for her.

"There, I did my part," Laura said and released Julie. "Now I'll leave you two to say your hellos or good-byes or whatevers." In the next instant she had disappeared back into the crowd, leaving Julie alone with Jeff. There was an uncomfortable moment of silence before they both spoke at once, then, at the same time, broke off.

"You first," Jeff said.

"I was only going to say that I didn't think you were here."

"And I was going to say that I didn't think you'd speak to me."

"Why shouldn't I?"

"You mean, knowing what I did and how it affected your dad, you'd still talk to me?"

Julie hesitated. Finally she said, "I've had a lot of time to think about that. I know you did what you thought was right, and, to tell you the truth, I'm not so sure you were wrong."

Jeff's eyebrows lifted. "Oh?"

"Well, I've heard about all the changes they're going to make at the lab, so I guess that's as good as an admission that things were pretty bad there."

Jeff nodded. "How does your dad feel about it?"

"Well, he'd never admit it, but I think all the bad publicity

213

made him take a good look at what he was doing. He's accepted a position back East at a primate research center where they're trying to foster normal social behavior among monkeys."

"No kidding. That's great." He paused a moment, then said, "How soon are you moving back there?"

"The day after graduation."

"Too bad," he said with a wry smile. "Given a little more time, I might have made a convert out of you."

"In some ways, you have."

"Only in some ways?"

"Well, someone always has to play devil's advocate, don't they?"

"I suppose," he said wistfully, shifting from one foot to the other. "No hard feelings?"

"None."

He shifted again. "Well, I just wanted to wish you good luck at Yale."

"But I'm going to Stanford."

He stared at her, a dumbfounded expression on his face. "I don't believe it."

"It's true."

His face broke into a big smile. "Hey, I'm going to Stanford too!"

Now she stared at him, looking just as astounded. "You really did it."

"Yes. And you know what made me decide?"

She shook her head.

"It was what you said about how I might regret it for the rest of my life if I didn't give it a try."

So he had actually taken the step. And she'd had something to do with it. Perhaps her year in Santa Delores hadn't been wasted after all. "That's really wonderful," she said. "And strange."

"Strange?"

"Yes. Something *you* said helped me decide too. That day we went to see Mercedes—afterward, at the creek, you pretty much said I did what everyone expected of me instead of what I wanted to do. I got to thinking that you were right, so, you see, you had a lot to do with my decision too."

"How *about* that!" he said.

"Weird," she said. "I mean, our coming to the same decision at the same time."

"And in the same way." They stared at each other in wonder, then Jeff beamed at her. "Fate seems to want to throw us together." He gave an exaggerated shrug of helplessness. "You can't fight fate."

"No," she agreed with a smile. "You can't fight fate."

Jeff said, "How are you at writing letters?"

"I write wonderful letters."

"Good. We'll correspond this summer. Then it won't seem so long until we see each other next term. Do you know where you'll be living at Stanford?"

They went on talking and talking about their plans for a new life. For Julie, the day had changed from depressing to radiant. She did, indeed, have a voice in her own destiny, and she was learning how to use it. She suspected the same was true for Jeff.

Afterword

Although this is a book of fiction, the animal experiments depicted, as well as all descriptions of the use and treatment of animals, are authentic, taken from many well-documented sources. Even the slaughter of the lamb took place in a California high school.

The laboratory—a composite—I have fashioned from a description by animal rights groups of the conditions they found in two of the labs they raided.

The rescued monkey, whose real name is Britches, does, indeed, live with a surrogate mother. The scars on his eyes are still evident.

I have changed only the names.

MILDRED AMES